James Smith

An Account of the Remarkable Occurrences in the Life and Travels

of Colonel James Smith

James Smith

An Account of the Remarkable Occurrences in the Life and Travels of Colonel James Smith

ISBN/EAN: 9783337292836

Printed in Europe, USA, Canada, Australia, Japan

Cover: Foto ©Raphael Reischuk / pixelio.de

More available books at **www.hansebooks.com**

AN ACCOUNT

OF THE

REMARKABLE OCCURRENCES

IN THE LIFE AND TRAVELS OF

Col. JAMES SMITH,

(Now a Citizen of Bourbon County, Kentucky,)

DURING HIS CAPTIVITY WITH THE INDIANS,

IN THE YEARS 1755, '56, '57, '58, & '59,

In which the Cuftoms, Manners, Traditions, Theological Sentiments, Mode of Warfare, Military Tactics, Difcipline and Encampments, Treatment of Prifoners, &c. are better explained, and more minutely related, than has been heretofore done, by any author on that fubject. Together with a Defcription of the Soil, Timber and Waters, where he travelled with the Indians, during his captivity.

TO WHICH IS ADDED,

A Brief Account of fome Very Uncommon Occurrences, which tranfpired after his return from captivity; as well as of the Different Campaigns carried on againft the Indians to the weftward of Fort Pitt, fince the year 1755, to the prefent date.

WRITTEN BY HIMSELF.

LEXINGTON:

PRINTED BY JOHN BRADFORD, ON MAIN STREET,

1799.

PREFACE.

I WAS ſtrongly urged to publiſh the following work, immediately after my return from captivity, which was nearly forty years ago—but, as at that time the Americans were ſo little acquainted with Indian affairs, I apprehended a great part of it would be viewed as fable or romance.

As the Indians never attempted to prevent me either from reading or writing, I kept a Journal, which I reviſed ſhortly after my return from captivity, and which I have kept ever ſince : and as I have had but a moderate Engliſh education, have been adviſed to employ ſome perſon of liberal education to tranſcribe and embelliſh it—but believing that nature always outſhines art, have thought, that occurrences truly and plainly ſtated, as they happened, would make the beſt hiſtory, be better underſttood, and moſt entertaining.

In the different Indian ſpeeches copied into this work, I have not only imitated their own ſtyle, or mode of ſpeaking, but have also preſerved the ideas meant to be communicated in those ſpeeches—In common converſation, I have uſed my own ſtyle, but preſerved their ideas. The principal advantage that I expect will reſult to the public, from the publication of the following ſheets, is the *obſervations on the Indian mode of warfare.* Experience has taught the Americans the neceſſity of adopting their mode, and the more perfect we are in that mode, the better we ſhall be able to defend ourſelves againſt them, when defence is neceſſary.

JAMES SMITH.

Bourbon County, June 1ſt, 1799.

REMARKABLE

OCCURRENCES, ETC.

IN May 1755, the province of Pennſylvania, agreed
to ſend out three hundred men, in order to cut a
waggon road from Fort Loudon, to join Braddock's
road, near the Turkey Foot, or three forks of Yoho-
gania. My brother-in-law, William Smith eſq. of Conococheague, was appointed commiſſioner, to have the
overſight of theſe road-cutters.

Though I was at that time only eighteen years of
age, I had fallen violently in love with a young lady,
whom I apprehended was poſſeſſed of a large ſhare of
both beauty and virtue; but being born between Venus
and Mars, I concluded I muſt alſo leave my dear fair
one, and go out with this company of road-cutters, to

fee the event of this campaign; but ftill expecting that fome time in the courfe of this fummer, I fhould again return to the arms of my beloved.

We went on with the road, without interruption, until near the Allegheny Mountain; when I was fent back, in order to hurry up fome provifion waggons that were on the way after us; I proceeded down the road as far as the croffings of Juniata, where, finding the waggons were coming on as faft as poffible, I returned up the road again towards the Allegheny Mountain, in company with one Arnold Vigoras. About four or five miles above Bedford, three Indians had made a blind of bufhes, ftuck in the ground, as though they grew naturally, where they concealed themfelves, about fifteen yards from the road. When we came oppofite to them, they fired upon us, at this fhort diftance, and killed my fellow traveller, yet their bullets did not touch me; but my horfe making a violent ftart, threw me, and the Indians immediately ran up, and took me prifoner. The one that laid hold on me was a Canafatauga, the other two were Delawares. One of them could fpeak Englifh, and afked me if there were any more white men coming after? I told them not any near, that I knew of. Two of thefe Indians ftood by me, whilft the other fcalped my comrade: they then fet off and ran at a fmart rate, through the woods, for about fifteen miles, and that night we flept on the Alegheny Mountain, without fire.

The next morning they divided the laft of their provifion which they had brought from Fort DuQuefne,
and gave me an equal fhare, which was about two or
three ounces of mouldy bifcuit—this and a young
Ground-Hog, about as large as a Rabbit, roafted, and
alfo equally divided, was all the provifion we had until
we came to the Loyal-Hannan, which was about fifty
miles; and a great part of the way we came through
exceeding rocky Laurel-thickets, without any path.
When we came to the Weft fide of Laurel Hill, they
gave the fcalp halloo, as ufual, which is a long yell or
halloo, for every fcalp or prifoner they have in poffeffion;
the laft of thefe fcalp halloos was followed with quick
and fudden, fhrill fhouts of joy and triumph.   On their
performing this, we were anfwered by the firing of a
number of guns on the Loyal-Hannan, one after another, quicker than one could count, by another party
of Indians, who were encampcd near where Ligoneer
now ftands.   As we advanced near this party, they
increafed with repeated fhouts of joy and triumph; but
I did not fhare with them in their exceffive mirth.
When we came to this camp, we found they had plenty
of Turkeys and other meat, there; and though I never
before eat venifon without bread or falt, yet as I was
hungry, it relifhed very well.   There we lay that night,
and the next morning the whole of us marched on our
way for Fort DuQuefne.   The night after we joined
another camp of Indians, with nearly the fame cere-

mony, attended with great noife, and apparent joy,
among all, except one. The next morning we continued
our march, and in the afternoon we came in full view of
the fort, which ftood on the point, near where Fort Pitt
now ftands. We then made a halt on the bank of the
Alegheny, and repeated the fcalp halloo, which was
anfwered by the firing of all the firelocks in the hands
of both Indians and French who were in and about the
fort, in the aforefaid manner, and alfo the great guns,
which were followed by the continued fhouts and yells
of the different favage tribes who were then collected
there.

As I was at this time unacquainted with this mode
of firing and yelling of the favages, I concluded that
there were thoufands of Indians there, ready to receive
General Braddock; but what added to my furprize, I
faw numbers running towards me, ftripped naked, excepting breech-clouts, and painted in the moft hideous
manner, of various colors, though the principal color
was vermillion, or a bright red; yet there was annexed
to this, black, brown, blue, &c. As they approached,
they formed themfelves into two long ranks, about two
or three rods apart. I was told by an Indian that
could fpeak Englifh, that I muft run betwixt thefe
ranks, and that they would flog me all the way, as I
ran, and if I ran quick, it would be fo much the better,
as they would quit when I got to the end of the ranks.
There appeared to be a general rejoicing around me,

yet I could find nothing like joy in my breaſt; but I
ſtarted to the race with all the reſolution and vigor I
was capable of exerting, and found that it was as I had
had been told, for I was flogged the whole way. When
I had got near the end of the lines, I was ſtruck with
ſomething that appeared to me to be a ſtick, or the
handle of a tommahawk, which cauſed me to fall to the
ground. On my recovering my ſenſes, I endeavored to
renew my race; but as I aroſe, ſome one caſt ſand in
my eyes, which blinded me ſo, that I could not ſee
where to run. They continued beating me moſt intolerably, until I was at length inſenſible; but before I
loſt my ſenſes, I remember my wiſhing them to ſtrike
the fatal blow, for I thought they intended killing me,
but apprehended they were too long about it.

The firſt thing I remember was my being in the fort,
amidſt the French and Indians, and a French doctor
ſtanding by me, who had opened a vein in my left arm:
after which the interpreter aſked me how I did, I told
him I felt much pain; the doctor then waſhed my
wounds, and the bruiſed places of my body, with
French brandy. As I felt faint, and the brandy ſmelt
well, I aſked for ſome inwardly, but the doctor told
me, by the interpreter, that it did not ſuit my caſe.

When they found I could ſpeak, a number of Indians
came around me, and examined me with threats of cruel
death, if I did not tell the truth. The firſt queſtion
they aſked me, was, how many men were there in the

2

party that were coming from Pennfylvania, to join
Braddock? I told them the truth, that there were
three hundred. The next queftion was, were they well
armed? I told them they were all well armed, (meaning the arm of flefh) for they had only about thirty
guns among the whole of them; which, if the Indians
had known, they would certainly have gone and cut
them all off; therefore I could not in confcience let
them know the defencelefs fituation of thefe road-cutters. I was then fent to the hofpital, and carefully
attended by the doctors, and recovered quicker than
what I expected.

Some time after I was there, I was vifited by the
Delaware Indian already mentioned, who was at the
taking of me, and could fpeak fome Englifh. Though
he fpoke but bad Englifh, yet I found him to be a man
of confiderable underftanding. I afked him if I had
done any thing that had offended the Indians, which
caufed them to treat me fo unmercifully? He faid no,
it was only an old cuftom the Indians had, and it was
like how do you do; after that he faid I would be well
ufed. I afked him if I fhould be admitted to remain
with the French? He faid no—and told me that as
foon as I recovered, I muft not only go with the Indians, but muft be made an Indian myfelf. I afked
him what news from Braddock's army? He faid the
Indians fpied them every day, and he fhewed me by
making marks on the ground with a ftick, that Brad-

dock's army was advancing in very clofe order, and that the Indians would furround them, take trees, and (as he exprefled it) *fhoot um down all one pigeon.*

Shortly after this, on the 9th day of July 1755, in the morning I heard a great ftir in the fort. As I could then walk with a ftaff in my hand, I went out of the door which was juft by the wall of the fort, and ftood upon the wall and viewed the Indians in a huddle before the gate, where were barrels of powder, bullets, flints &c., and every one taking what fuited; I faw the Indians alfo march off in rank intire—likewife the French Canadians, and fome regulars, after viewing the Indians and French in different pofitions, I computed them to be about four hundred, and wondered that they attempted to go out againft Braddock with fo fmall a party. I was then in high hopes that I would foon fee them flying before thc Britifh troops, and that General Braddock would take the fort and refcue me.

I remained anxious to know the event of this day; and in the afternoon I again obferved a great noife and commotion in the fort, and though at that time I could not underftand French, yet I found it was the voice of Joy and triumph, and feared that they had received what I called bad news.

I had obferved fome of the old country foldiers fpeak Dutch, as I fpoke Dutch I went to one of them and afked him what was the news? he told me that a runner had juft arrived, who faid that Braddock would

certainly be defeated; that the Indians and French had
furrounded him, and were concealed behind trees and in
gullies, and kept a conftant fire upon the Englifh, and
that they faw the Englifh falling in heaps, and if they
did not take the river which was the only gap, and
make their efcape, there would not be one man left
alive before fun down. Some time after this I heard a
number of fcalp halloo's and faw a company of Indians
and French coming in. I obferved they had a great
many bloody fcalps, grenadiers' caps, Britifh canteens,
bayonets &c. with them. They brought the news that
Braddock was defeated. After that another company
came in which appeared to be about one hundred, and
chiefly Indians, and it feemed to me that almoft every
one of this company was carrying fcalps; after this came
another company with a number of waggon-horfes, and
alfo a great many fcalps. Thofe that were coming in,
and thofe that had arrived, kept a conftant firing of
fmall arms, and alfo the great guns in the fort, which
were accompanied with the moft hedeous fhouts and
yells from all quarters; fo that it appeared to me as if
the infernal regions had broke loofe.

About fun down I beheld a fmall party coming in
with about a dozen prifoners, ftripped naked, with their
hands tied behind their backs, and their faces, and part
of their bodies blacked—thefe prifoners they burned to
death on the bank of Alegheny River oppofite to the
fort. I ftood on the fort wall until I beheld them begin

to burn one of thefe men, they had him tied to a ftake and kept touching him with fire-brands, red-hot irons &c. and he fcreeming in a moft doleful manner,—the Indians in the mean time yelling like infernal fpirits. As this fcene appeared too fhocking for me to behold, I retired to my lodging both fore and forry.

When I came into my lodgings I faw Ruffel's Seven Sermons, which they had brought from the field of battle, which a Frenchman made a prefent of to me. From the beft information I could receive there were only feven Indians and four French killed in this battle, and five hundred Britifh lay dead in the field ; befides what were killed in the river on their retreat.

The morning after the battle I faw Braddock's artilery brought into the fort, the fame day I alfo faw feveral Indians in Britifh-officers' drefs with fafh, half-moon, laced hats &c. which the Britifh then wore.

A few days after this the Indians demanded me and I was obliged to go with them. I was not yet well able to march, but they took me in a canoe, up the Alegheny River to an Indian town that was on the north fide of the river, about forty miles above Fort DuQuefne. Here I remained about three weeks, and was then taken to an Indian town on the weft branch of Mufkingum, about twenty miles above the forks, which was called Tullihas, inhabited by Delawares, Caughnewagas and Mohicans.—On our rout betwixt the aforefaid towns, the country was chiefly black-oak and white-oak land,

which appeared generally to be good wheat land, chiefly
fecond and third rate, intermixed with fome rich bottoms.

The day after my arrival at the aforefaid town, a
number of Indians collected about me, and one of them
began to pull the hair out of my head. He had fome
afhes on a piece of bark, in which he frequently diped
his fingers in order to take the firmer hold, and fo he
went on, as if he had been plucking a turkey, until he
had all the hair clean out of my head, except a fmall
fpot about three or four inches fquare on my crown;
this they cut off with a pair of fciffors, excepting three
locks, which they dreffed up in their own mode. Two
of thefe they wraped round with a narrow beaded garter
made by themfelves for that purpofe, and the other they
platted at full length, and then ftuck it full of filver
broches. After this they bored my nofe and ears, and
fixed me off with ear rings and nofe jewels, then they
ordered me to ftrip off my clothes and put on a breech-
clout, which I did; then they painted my head, face
and body in various colors. They put a large belt of
wampom on my neck, and filver bands on my hands
and right arm; and fo an old chief led me out in the
ftreet and gave the alarm halloo, *coo-wigh,* feveral times
repeated quick, and on this all that were in the town
came running and ftood round the old chief, who held
me by the hand in the midft. As I at that time knew
nothing of their mode of adoption, and had feen them
put to death all they had taken, and as I never could

find that they faved a man alive at Braddock's defeat, I made no doubt but they were about putting me to death in fome cruel manner. The old chief holding me by the hand made a long fpeech very loud, and when he had done he handed me to three young fquaws, who led me by the hand down the bank into the river until the water was up to our middle. The fquaws then made figns to me to plunge myfelf into the water, but I did not underftand them; I thought that the refult of the council was that I fhould be drowned, and that thefe young ladies were to be the executioners. They all three laid violent hold of me, and I for fome time oppofed them with all my might, which occafioned loud laughter by the multitude that were on the bank of the river. At length one of the fquaws made out to fpeak a little Englifh (for I believe they began to be afraid of me) and faid, *no hurt you;* on this I gave myfelf up to their ladyfhips, who were as good as their word; for though they plunged me under water, and wafhed and rubbed me feverely, yet I could not fay they hurt me much.

Thefe young women then led me up to the council houfe, where fome of the tribe were ready with new cloths for me. They gave me a new ruffled fhirt, which I put on, alfo a pair of leggins done off with ribbons and beads, likewife a pair of mockafons, and garters dreffed with beads, Porcupine-quills, and red hair—alfo a tinfel laced cappo. They again painted my head and face with various colors, and tied a bunch of red feathers to one of thefe locks they had left on the crown of my head, which ftood up five or fix inches. They feated me on a bear fkin, and gave me a pipe, tomahawk, and polecat fkin pouch, which had been fkined pocket fafhion, and contained tobacco, killegenico, or dry fumach leaves, which they mix with their tobacco,—alfo fpunk, flint and fteel. When I was thus feated, the Indians came in dreffed and painted in their grandeft manner. As they came in they took their feats and for a confiderable time there was a profound filence, every one was fmoking,—but not a word was fpoken among them.—At length one of the chiefs made a fpeech which was delivered to me by an interpreter,—and was as followeth :—" My fon, you are now flefh of our flefh, and bone of our bone. By the ceremony which was performed this day, every drop of white blood was wafhed out of your veins ; you are taken into the Caughnewago nation, and initiated into a warlike tribe ; you are adopted into a great family, and now received with great ferioufnefs and folemnity in the room and place of a great man ; after what has paffed this day, you are now one of us by an old ftrong law and cuftom—My fon, you have now nothing to fear, we are now under the fame obligations to love, fupport and defend you, that we are to love and defend one another, therefore you are to confider yourfelf as one of our people."—At this time I did not believe this fine fpeech, efpecially that of the white blood being wafhed out of me; but fince that time I have found that there was much fincerity in faid fpeech,—for from that day I never knew them to make any diftinction between me and themfelves in any refpect whatever until I left them.—If they had plenty of cloathing I had plenty, if we were fcarce we all fhared one fate.

After this ceremony was over, I was introduced to my new kin, and told that I was to attend a feaft that evening, which I did. And as the cuftom was, they gave me alfo a bowl and wooden fpoon, which I carried with me to the place, where there was a number of large brafs kettles full of boiled venifon and green corn; every one advanced with his bowl and fpoon and had his fhare given him.—After this, one of the chiefs made a fhort fpeech, and then we began to eat.

The name of one of the chiefs in this town was Tecanyaterighto, alias Pluggy, and the other Afallecoa alias Mohawk Solomon.—As Pluggy and his party were to ftart the next day to war, to the frontiers of Virginia, the next thing to be performed was the war dance, and their war fongs. At their war dance they had both vocal and inftrumental mufic. They had a fhort holow gum clofe in one end, with water in it, and parchment ftretched over the open end thereof, which they beat with one ftick, and made a found nearly like a muffled drum; all thofe who were going on this expedition collected together and formed. An old Indian then began

3

to fing and timed the mufic by beating on this drum, as the ancients formerly timed their mufic by beating the tabor. On this the warriors began to advance, or move forward in concert, like well difciplined troops would march to the fife and drum. Each warrior had a tomahawk, fpear or war-mallet in his hand, and they all moved regularly towards the eaft, or the way they intended to go to war. At length they all ftretched their tomahawks towards the Potomack, and giving a hideous fhout or yell, they wheeled quick about, and danced in the fame manner back. The next was the war fong. In performing this, only one fung at a time, in a moving pofture, with a tomahawk in his hand, while all the other warriors were engaged in calling aloud *he-uh*, *he-uh*, which they conftantly repeated, while the war fong was going on. When the warior that was finging had ended his fong, he ftruck a war poft with his tomahawk, and with a loud voice told what warlike exploits he had done, and what he now intended to do, which was anfwered by the other wariors, with loud fhouts of applaufe. Some who had not before intended to go to war, at this time were fo animated by this performance that they took up the tomahawk and fung the war fong, which was anfwered with fhouts of joy, as they were then initiated into the prefent marching company. The next morning this company all collected at one place, with their heads and faces painted with various colors, and packs upon their backs; they marched off all silent, except the commander, who, in the front sang the travelling song, which began in this manner: *hoo caughtainte heegana.* Just as the rear passed the end of the town, they began to fire in their slow manner, from the front to the rear, which was accompanied with shouts and yells from all quarters.

This evening I was invited to another sort of dance, which was a kind of promiscuous dance. The young men stood in one rank, and the young women in another, about one rod apart, facing each other. The one that raised the tune, or started the song, held a small gourd or dry shell of a squash, in his hand, which contained beads or small stones, which rattled. When he began to sing, he timed the tune with his rattle; both men and women danced and sung together, advancing towards each other, stooping until their heads would be touching together, and then ceased from dancing, with loud shouts, and retreated and formed again, and so repeated the same thing over and over, for three or four hours, without intermission. This exercise appeared to me at first irrational and insipid; but I found that in singing their tunes, they used *ya ne no hoo wa ne &c.,* like our *fa sol la,* and though they have no such thing as jingling verse, yet they can intermix sentences with their notes, and say what they please to each other, and carry on the tune in concert. I found that this was a kind of wooing or courting dance, and as they

advanced ftooping with their heads together, they could
fay what they pleafed in each other's ear, without difcon-
certing their rough mufic, and the others, or thofe near,
not hear what they fay.

Shortly after this I went out to hunt, in company with
Mohawk Solomon, fome of the Caughnewagas and a Delaware Indian that was married to a Caughnewaga fquaw.
We travelled about fouth, from this town, and the firft
night we killed nothing, but we had with us green corn,
which we roafted and ate that night.   The next day we
encamped about twelve o'clock, and the hunters turned
out to hunt, and I went down the run that we encamped
on, in company with fome fquaws and boys, to hunt
plumbs, which we found in great plenty. On my
return to camp I obferved a large piece of fat meat: the
Delaware Indian that could talk fome Englifh, obferved
me looking earneftly at this meat, and afked me *what
meat you think that is?*   I faid I fuppofed it was bear
meat; he laughed and faid, *ho, all one fool you, beal now
elly pool*, and pointing to the other fide of the camp, he
faid *look at that fkin, you think that beal fkin?* I went and
lifted the fkin, which appeared like an ox hide: he then
faid, *what fkin you think that?*   I replied that I thought
it was a buffaloe hide; he laughed and faid *you fool
again, you know nothing, you think buffaloe that colo?* I
acknowledged I did not know much about thefe things,
and told him I never faw a buffaloe, and that I had not
heard what color they were. He replied *by and by you*

ſhall ſee gleat many buffaloe; He now go to gleat lick. That ſkin no buffaloe ſkin, that ſkin buck-elk ſkin. They went out with horſes, and brought in the remainder of this buck-elk which was the fatteſt creature I ever ſaw of the tallow kind.

We remained at this camp about eight or ten days, and killed a number of deer. Though we had neither bread or ſalt at this time, yet we had both roaſt and boiled meat in great plenty, and they were frequently inviting me to eat, when I had no appetite.

We then moved to the buffaloe lick, where we killed ſeveral buffaloe, and in their ſmall braſs kettles they made about half a buſhel of ſalt. I ſuppoſe this lick was about thirty or forty miles from the aforeſaid town, and ſomewhere between the Muſkingum, Ohio and Sciota. About the lick was clear, open woods, and thin white-oak land, and at that time there were large roads leading to the lick, like waggon roads. We moved from this lick about ſix or ſeven miles, and encamped on a creek.

Though the Indians had given me a gun, I had not yet been admitted to go out from the camp to hunt. At this place Mohawk Solomon aſked me to go out with him to hunt, which I readily agreed to. After ſome time we came upon ſome freſh buffaloe tracks. I had obſerved before this that the Indians were upon their guard, and afraid of an enemy; for, until now they and the ſouthern nations had been at war. As we were fol-

lowing the buffaloe tracks, Solomon feemed to be upon
his guard, went very flow, and would frequently ftand
and liften, and appeared to be in fufpenfe. We came
to where the tracks were very plain in the fand, and I
faid it is furely buffaloe tracks; he faid *hufh, you know
nothing, may be buffaloe tracks, may be Catawba.* He
went very cautious until we found fome frefh buffaloe
dung: he then fmiled and faid *Catawba can not make fo.*
He then ftopped and told me an odd ftory about the
Catawbas. He faid that formerly the Catawbas came
near one of their hunting camps, and at fome diftance
from the camp lay in ambufh, and in order to decoy
them out, fent two or three Catawbas in the night, paft
their camp, with buffaloe hoofs fixed on their feet, fo as
to make artificial tracks. In the morning thofe in the
camp followed after thefe tracks, thinking they were
Buffaloe, until they were fired on by the Catawbas, and
feveral of them killed; the others fled, collected a party
and purfued the Catawbas; but they, in their fubtilty
brought with them rattle-fnake poifon, which they had
collected from the bladder that lieth at the root of the
fnakes' teeth; this they had corked up in a fhort piece of
cane-ftalk; they had alfo brought with them fmall cane
or reed, about the fize of a rye ftraw, which they made
fharp at the end like a pen, and dipped them in this
poifon, and ftuck them in the ground among the grafs,
along their own tracks, in fuch a pofition that they
might ftick into the legs of the purfuers, which anfwered

the defign ; and as the Catawbas had runners behind to watch the motions of the purfuers, when they found that a number of them were lame, being artificially fnake bit, and that they were all turning back, the Catawbas turned upon the purfuers, and defeated them, and killed and fcalped all those that were lame.—When Solomon had finifhed this ftory, and found that I underftood him, concluded by faying, *you don't know, Catawba velly bad Indian, Catawba all one Devil Catawba.*

Some time after this, I was told to take the dogs with me and go down the creek, perhaps I might kill a turkey ; it being in the afternoon, I was alfo told not to go far from the creek, and to come up the creek again to the camp, and to take care not to get loft. When I had gone fome diftance down the creek I came upon frefh buffaloe tracks, and as I had a number of dogs with me to ftop the buffaloe, I concluded I would follow after and kill one; and as the grafs and weeds were rank, I could readily follow the track. A little before fundown, I defpaired of coming up with them : I was then thinking how I might get to camp before night ; I concluded as the buffaloe had made feveral turns, if I took the track back to the creek, it would be dark before I could get to camp ; therefore I thought I would take a near way through the hills, and ftrike the creek a little below the camp ; but as it was cloudy weather, and I a very young woodfman, I could find neither creek or camp. When night came on I fired my gun feveral times, and hallooed, but could have no anfwer. The next morning early, the Indians were out after me, and as I had with me ten or a dozen dogs, and the grafs and weeds rank, they could readily follow my track. When they came up with me, they appeared to be in a very good humor. I afked Solomon if he thought I was running away, he faid *no no, you go too much clooked.* On my return to camp they took my gun from me, and for this rafh ftep I was reduced to a bow and arrows, for near two years. We were out on this tour about fix weeks.

This country is generally hilly, though intermixed with confiderable quantities of rich upland, and fome good bottoms.

When we returned to the town, Pluggy and his party had arrived, and brought with them a confiderable number of fcalps and prifoners from the South Branch of Potomack: they alfo brought with them an Englifh Bible, which they gave to a Dutch woman who was a prifoner; but as fhe could not read Englifh, fhe made a prefent of it to me, which was very acceptable.

I remain in this town until fome time in October, when my adopted brother called Tontileaugo, who had married a Wiandot fquaw, took me with him to Lake Erie. We proceeded up the weft branch of Mufkingum, and for fome diftance up the river the land was hilly but intermixed with large bodies of tolerable rich upland, and excellent bottoms. We proceeded on, to the head waters of the weſt branch of Muſkingum. On the head waters of this branch, and from thence to the waters of Caneſadooharie, there is a large body of rich, well lying land—the timber is aſh, walnut, ſugar-tree, buckeye, honey-locuſt and cherry, intermixed with ſome oak, hickory, &c.—This tour was at the time that the black-haws were ripe, and we were ſeldom out of ſight of them : they were common here both in the bottoms and upland.

On this route we had no horſes with us, and when we ſtarted from the town, all the pack I carried was a pouch, containing my books, a little dried veniſon, and my blanket. I had then no gun, but Tontileaugo who was a firſt rate hunter, carried a rifle gun, and every day killed deer, racoons or bears. We left the meat, excepting a little for preſent uſe, and carried the ſkins with us until we encamped, and then ſtretched them with elm bark, in a frame made with poles ſtuck in the ground and tied together with lynn or elm bark; and when the ſkins were dried by the fire, we packed them up, and carried them with us the next day.

As Tontileaugo could not ſpeak Engliſh, I had to make uſe of all the Caughnewaga I had learned even to talk very imperfeꞓly with him : but I found I learned to talk Indian faſter this way, than when I had thoſe with me who could ſpeak Engliſh.

As we proceeded down the Caneſadooharie waters, our packs encreaſed by the ſkins that were daily killed, and became so very heavy that we could not march more than eight or ten miles per day. We came to Lake Erie about six miles west of the mouth of Canesadooharie. As the wind was very high the evening we came to the Lake, I was surprized to hear the roaring of the water, and see the high waves that dashed against the shore, like the Ocean. We encamped on a run near the lake; and as the wind fell that night, the next morning the lake was only in a moderate motion, and we marched on the sand along the side of the water, frequently resting ourselves, as we were heavy laden. I saw on the strand a number of large fish, that had been left in flat or hollow places; as the wind fell and the waves abated, they were left without water, or only a small quantity; and numbers of Bald and Grey Eagles, &c. were along the shore devouring them.

Some time in the afternoon we came to a large camp of Wiandots, at the mouth of Canesadooharie, where Tontileaugo's wife was. Here we were kindly received: they gave us a kind of rough, brown potatoes, which grew spontaneously and is called by the Caughnewagas *ohnenata*. These potatoes peeled and dipped in racoon's fat, taste nearly like our sweet-potatoes. They also gave us what they call *caneheanta*, which is a kind of hominy, made of green corn, dried, and beans mixed together.

From the head waters of Canesadooharie to this place, the land is generally good; chiefly first or second rate, and, comparatively, little or no third rate. The only refuſe is ſome ſwamps, that appear to be too wet for uſe, yet I apprehend that a number of them, if drained, would make excellent meadows. The timber is black-oak, walnut, hickory, cherry, black-aſh, white-aſh, water-aſh, buckeye, black-locuſt, honey-locuſt, ſugar-tree, and elm: there is alſo ſome land, though, comparatively, but ſmall, where the timber is chiefly white-oak or beach— this may be called third rate. In the bottoms, and alſo many places in the upland, there is a large quantity of wild apple, plumb, and red and black-haw trees. It appeared to be well watered, and a plenty of meadow ground, intermixed with upland, but no large prairies or glades, that I ſaw, or heard of. In this route, deer, bear, turkeys, and racoons, appeared plenty, but no buffaloe, and very little ſign of elks.

We continued our camp at the mouth of Caneſadoo-harie for ſome time, where we killed ſome deer, and a great many racoons; the racoons here were remarka-bly large and fat.—At length we all embarked in a large birch bark canoe. This veſſel was about four feet wide, and three feet deep, and about five and thirty feet long: and tho it could carry a heavy burden, it was ſo artfully and curiouſly conſtructed that four men could cary it ſeveral miles, or from one landing place to an-other, or from the waters of the Lake to the waters of the Ohio.—We proceeded up Caneſadooharie a few miles and went on ſhore to hunt; but to my great furprife they carried the veffel that we all came in up the bank, and inverted it or turned the bottom up, and converted it to a dwelling houfe, and kindled a fire before us to warm ourfelves by and cook. With our baggage and ourfelves in this houfe we were very much crouded, yet our little houfe turned off the rain very well.

We kept moving and hunting up this river until we came to the falls; here we remained fome weeks, and killed a number of deer, feveral bears, and a great many racoons. From the mouth of this river to the falls is about five and twenty miles. On our paffage up I was not much out from the river, but what I faw was good land, and not hilly.

About the falls is thin chefnut land, which is almoft the only chefnut timber I ever faw in this country.

While we remained here, I left my pouch with my books in camp, wrapt up in my blanket, and went out to hunt chefnuts. On my return to camp my books were miffing. I enquired after them, and afked the Indians if they knew where they were; they told me that they fuppofed the puppies had carried them off. I did not believe them; but thought they were difpleafed at my poring over my books, and concluded that they had deftroyed them, or put them out of my way.

After this I was again out after nuts, and on my return beheld a new erection, which were two white oak faplings, that were forked about twelve feet high, and

ſtood about fifteen feet apart. They had cut theſe ſap-
lings at the forks and laid a ſtrong pole acroſs which
appeared in the form of a gallows, and the poſts they
had ſhaved very ſmooth and painted in places with ver-
milion. I could not conceive the uſe of this piece of
work, and at length concluded it was a gallows, I
thought that I had diſpleaſed them by reading my
books, and that they were about puting me to death.—
The next morning I obſerved them bringing their ſkins
all to this place and hanging them over this pole, ſo as
to preſerve them from being injured by the weather,
this removed my fears. They alſo buried their large
canoe in the ground, which is the way they took to preſerve this ſort of a canoe in the winter ſeaſon.

As we had at this time no horſes, every one got a
pack on his back, and we ſteered an eaſt courſe about
twelve miles, and encamped. The next morning we
proceeded on the ſame courſe about ten miles to a large
creek that empties into Lake Erie betwixt Caneſadooharie, and Cayahaga. Here they made their winter
cabbin, in the following form. They cut logs about
fifteen feet long, and laid theſe logs upon each other,
and drove poſts in the ground at each end to keep them
together; the poſts they tied together at the top with
bark, and by this means raiſed a wall fifteen feet long,
and about four feet high, and in the ſame manner they
raiſed another wall oppoſite to this, at about twelve feet
diſtance; then they drove forks in the ground in the

centre of each end, and laid a ſtrong pole from end to end on theſe forks; and from theſe walls to the poles, they ſet up poles inſtead of rafters, and on theſe they tied ſmall poles in place of laths; and a cover was made of lynn bark which will run even in the winter ſeaſon.

As every tree will not run, they examine the tree firſt, by trying it near the ground, and when they find it will do, they fall the tree and raiſe the bark with the toma-hawk, near the top of the tree about five or ſix inches broad, then put the tomahawk handle under this bark, and pull it along down to the butt of the tree; ſo that ſome times one piece of bark will be thirty feet long; this bark they cut at ſuitable lengths in order to cover the hut.

At the end of theſe walls they ſet up ſplit timber, ſo that they had timber all round, excepting a door at each end. At the top, in place of a chimney, they left an open place, and for bedding they laid down the afore-ſaid kind of bark, on which they ſpread bear ſkins. From end to end of this hut along the middle there were fires, which the ſquaws made of dry ſplit wood, and the holes or open places that appeared, the ſquaws ſtopped with moſs, which they collected from old logs; and at the door they hung a bear ſkin; and notwith-ſtanding the winters are hard here, our lodging was much better than what I expected.

It was ſome time in December when we finiſhed this winter cabin; but when we had got into this comparatively fine lodging, another difficulty arofe, we had nothing to eat. While I was travelling with Tontil-eaugo, as was before mentioned, and had plenty of fat venifon, bears meat and racoons, I then thought it was hard living without bread or Salt; but now I began to conclude that if I had anything that would banifh pinching hunger, and keep foul and body together I would be content.

While the hunters were all out, exerting themfelves to the utmoft of their ability, the fquaws and boys (in which clafs I was) were fcattered out in the bottoms, hunting red-haws, black-haws and hickory-nuts. As it was too late in the year, we did not fucceed in gathering haws, but we had tolerable fuccefs in fcratching up hickory-nuts from under a light fnow, which we carried with us left the hunters fhould not fucceed. After our return the hunters came in, who had killed only two fmall turkeys, which were but little among eight hunters and thirteen fquaws, boys and children;—but they were divided with the greateft equity and juftice—every one got their equal fhare.

The next day the hunters turned out again, and killed one deer and three bears.

One of the bears was very large and remarkably fat. The hunters carried in meat fufficient to give us all a hearty fupper and breakfaft.

The fquaws and all that could carry turned out to bring in meat, every one had their fhare affigned them, and my load was among the leaft; yet, not being accustomed to carrying in this way, I got exceeding weary, and told them that my load was too heavy, I muſt leave part of it and come for it again. They made a halt and only laughed at me, and took part of my load and added it to a young ſquaw's, who had as much before as I carried.

This kind of reproof had a great tendency to excite me to exert myſelf in carrying without complaining, than if they had whipped me for lazineſs. After this the hunters held a council and concluded that they muſt have horſes to carry their loads; and that they would go to war even in this inclement ſeaſon, in order to bring in horſes.

Tontileaugo wiſhed to be one of thoſe who ſhould go to war; but the votes went againſt him, as he was one of our beſt hunters; it was thought neceſſary to to leave him at this winter camp to provide for the ſquaws and children; it was agreed upon that Tontileaugo and three others ſhould ſtay and hunt, and the other four go to war.

They then began to go through their common ceremony. They ſung their war ſongs danced their war dances &c. And when they were equipped they went off ſinging their marching ſongs and firing their guns. Our camp appeared to be rejoicing; but I was grieved to think that ſome innocent perſons would be murdered not thinking of danger.

After the departure of theſe warriors we had hard times, and tho we were not altogether out of proviſions we were brought to ſhort allowance. At length Tontileaugo had confiderable fuccefs; and we had meat brought into camp fufficient to laft ten days. Tontileaugo then took me with him in order to encamp fome diftance from this winter cabbin, to try his luck there. We carried no provifion with us, he faid we would leave what was there for the fquaws and children, and that we could fhift for ourfelves. We fteered about a fouth courfe up the waters of this creek, and encamped about ten or twelve miles from the winter cabbin. As it was ftill cold weather and a cruft upon the fnow, which made a noife as we walked and alarmed the deer, we could kill nothing, and confequently went to fleep without fupper. The only chance we had under thefe circumftances, was to hunt bear holes; as the bears about Chriftmas fearch out a winter lodging place, where they lie about three or four months without eating or drinking. This may appear to fome incredible; but it is now well known to be the cafe, by thofe who live in the remote weftern parts of North America.

The next morning early we proceeded on, and when we found a tree fcratched by the bears climbing up, and the hole in the tree fufficiently large for the reception of the bear; we then fell a fapling or fmall tree againft or near the hole; and it was my bufinefs to climb up and drive out the bear, while Tontileaugo ftood ready with his gun and bow. We went on in this manner until evening, without fuccefs; at length we found a large elm fcratched, and a hole in it about forty feet up; but no tree nigh fuitable to lodge againft the hole. Tontileaugo got a long pole and fome dry rotten wood which he tied in bunches, with bark, and as there was a tree that grew near the elm, and extended up near the hole; but leaned the wrong way; fo that we could not lodge it to advantage; but to remedy this inconvenience, he climed up this tree and carried with him his rotten wood, fire and pole. The rotten wood he tied to his belt, and to one end of the pole he tied a hook, and a piece of rotten wood which he fet fire to, as it would retain fire almoft like fpunk; and reached this hook from limb to limb as he went up; when he got up, with this pole he put dry wood on fire into the hole, after he put in the fire he heard the bear fnuff and he came fpeedily down, took his gun in his hand and waited until the bear would come out; but it was fome time before it appeared, and when it did appear he attempted taking fight with his rifle, but it being then too dark to fee the fights, he fet it down by a tree, and inftantly bent his bow, took hold of an arrow, and fhot the bear a little behind the fhoulder; I was preparing alfo to fhoot an arrow, but he called to me to ftop, there was no occafion; and with that the bear fell to the ground.

Being very hungry we kindled a fire, opened the bear, took out the liver, and wrapped fome of the caul fat round and put it on a wooden fpit which we ftuck in the ground by the fire to roaft, we then fkinned the bear, got on our kettle, and had both roaft and boiled, and alfo fauce to our meat, which appeared to me to be delicate fare. After I was fully fatisfied I went to fleep, Tontileaugo awoke me, faying, come eat hearty, we have got meat plenty now.

The next morning we cut down a lynn tree, peeled bark and made a fnug little fhelter, facing the fouth eaft, with a large log betwixt us and the north weft; we made a good fire before us, and fcaffolded up our meat at one fide.—When we had finifhed our camp we went out to hunt, fearched two trees for bears, but to no purpofe. As the fnow thawed a little in the afternoon Tontileaugo killed a deer, which we carried with us to camp.

The next day we turned out to hunt, and near the camp we found a tree well fcratched; but the hole was above forty feet high, and no tree that we could lodge againft the hole; but finding that it was very hollow, we concluded that we would cut down the tree with our tomahawks, which kept us working a confiderable part of the day. When the tree fell we ran up, Tontileaugo with his gun and bow, and I with my bow ready bent. Tontileaugo fhot the bear through with his rifle, a little behind the fhoulders, I alfo fhot, but too far back; and not being then much accuftomed to the bufinefs, my arrow penetrated only a few inches thro the fkin. Having killed an old fhe bear and three cubs, we hawled her on the fnow to the camp, and only had time afterwards, to get wood, make a fire, cook &c. before dark.

Early the next morning we went to bufinefs, fearched feveral trees, but found no bears. On our way home we took three racoons out of a hollow elm, not far from the ground.

We remained here about two weeks, and in this time killed four bears, three deer, feveral turkeys, and a number of racoons. We packed up as much meat as we could carry, and returned to our winter cabin. On our arrival, there was great joy, as they were all in a ftarving condition,—the three hunters that we had left having killed but very little.—All that could carry a pack repaired to our camp to bring in meat.

Some time in February the four warriors returned, who had taken two fcalps, and fix horfes from the fron-tiers, of Pennfylvania. The hunters could then fcatter out a confiderable diftance from the winter cabin, and encamp, kill meat and pack it in upon horfes; fo that we commonly after this had plenty of provifion.

In this month we began to make fugar. As fome of the elm bark will ftrip at this feafon, the fquaws after finding a tree that would do, cut it down, and with a crooked ftick broad and fharp at the end, took the bark off the tree, and of this bark, made veffels in a curious manner, that would hold about two gallons each: they made above one hundred of thefe kind of veffels. In the fugar-tree they cut a notch, flooping down, and at the end of the notch, ftuck in a tomahawk; in the place where they ftuck the tomahawk, they drove a long chip, in order to carry the water out from the tree, and under this they fet their veffel, to receive it. As fugar trees were plenty and large here, they feldom or never notched a tree that was not two or three feet over. They alfo made bark veffels for carrying the water, that would hold about four gallons each. They had two brafs kettles, that held about fifteen gallons each, and other fmaller kettles in which they boiled the water. But as they could not at all times boil away the water as faft as it was collected, they made veffels of bark, that would hold about one hundred gallons each, for retaining the water; and tho' the fugar trees did not run every day, they had always a fufficient quantity of water to keep them boiling during the whole fugar feafon.

The way that we commonly ufed our fugar while en-camped, was by putting it in bears fat until the fat was almoft as fweet as the fugar itfelf, and in this we dipped our roafted venifon. About this time fome of the Indian lads and myfelf, were employed in making and attending traps for catching racoons, foxes, wild cats, &c.

As the racoon is a kind of water animal, that fre-quents the runs, or fmall water-courfes, almoft the whole night, we made our traps on the runs, by laying one fmall fapling on another, and driving in pofts to keep them from rolling. The upper fapling we raifed about eighteen inches, and fet fo, that on the racoons touching a ftring, or fmall piece of bark, the fapling would fall and kill it; and left the racoon fhould pafs by, we laid brufh on both fides of the run, only leaving the channel open.

The fox traps we made nearly in the fame manner, at the end of a hollow log, or oppofite to a hole at the root of a hollow tree, and put venifon on a ftick for bait: we had it fo fet that when the fox took hold of the meat, the trap fell. While the fquaws were employed in making fugar, the boys and men were engaged in hunting and trapping.

About the latter end of March we began to prepare for moving into town, in order to plant corn: the fquaws were then frying the laft of their bears fat, and making veffels to hold it: the veffels were made of deer fkins, which were fkinned by pulling the fkin off the neck, without ripping. After they had taken off the hair, they gathered it in fmall plaits round the neck and with a ftring drew it together like a purfe: in the centre a pin was put, below which they tied a ftring, and while it was wet they blew it up like a bladder, and let it remain in this manner, until it was dry, when it appeared nearly in the fhape of a fugar loaf, but more rounding at the lower end. One of thefe veffels would hold about four or five gallons; in thefe veffels it was they carried their bears oil.

When all things were ready we moved back to the falls of Canefadooharie. In this route the land is chiefly firft and fecond rate, but too much meadow ground, in proportion to the up land. The timber is white-aſh, elm, black-oak, cherry, buckeye, ſugar-tree, lynn, mulberry, beech, white-oak, hickory, wild apple-tree, red-haw, black-haw, and ſpicewood buſhes. There is in ſome places, ſpots of beech timber, which ſpots may be called third rate land. Buckeye, ſugar-tree, and ſpicewood, are common in the woods here. There is in ſome places, large ſwamps too wet for any uſe.

On our arrival at the falls, (as we had brought with us on horſe back, about two hundred weight of ſugar, a large quantity of bears oil, ſkins, &c.) the canoe we had buried was not ſufficient to carry all; therefore we were obliged to make another one of elm bark. While we lay here a young Wiandot found my books: on this they collected together; I was a little way from the camp, and ſaw the collection, but did not know what it meant. They called me by my Indian name, which was Scoouwa, repeatedly. I ran to ſee what was the matter, they ſhewed me my books, and ſaid they were glad they had been found, for they knew I was grieved at the loſs of them, and that they now rejoiced with me becauſe they were found. As I could then ſpeak ſome Indian, eſpecially Caughnewaga (for both that and the Wiandot tongue were ſpoken in this camp) I told them that I thanked them for the kindneſs they had always ſhewn to me, and alſo for finding my books. They aſked if the books were damaged? I told them not much. They then ſhewed how they lay, which was in the best manner to turn off the water. In a deer-skin pouch they lay all winter. The print was not much injured, though the binding was.—This was the first time that I felt my heart warm towards the Indians. Though they had been exceeding kind to me, I still before detested them, on account of the barbarity I beheld after Braddock's defeat. Neither had I ever before pretended kindness, or expressed myelf in a friendly manner; but I began now to excuse the Indians on account of their want of information.

When we were ready to embark, Tontileaugo would not go to town, but go up the river and take a hunt. He asked me if I choosed to go with him? I told him I did. We then got some sugar, bears oil bottled up in a bear's gut, and some dry venison, which we packed up, and went up Canesadooharie, about thirty miles, and encamped. At this time I did not know either the day of the week or the month; but I supposed it to be about the first of April. We had confiderable success in our business. We also found some stray horses, or a horse, mare, and a young colt; and though they had run in the woods all winter, they were in exceeding good order. There is plenty of grass here all winter, under the snow, and horses accustomed to the woods can work it out.—These horses had run in the woods until they were very wild.

Tontileaugo one night concluded that we must run them down. I told him I thought we could not accomplifh it. He faid he had run down bears, buffaloes and elks: and in the great plains, with only a fmall fnow on the ground, he had run down a deer; and he thought that in one whole day, he could tire, or run down any four footed animal except a wolf. I told him that though a deer was the fwifteft animal to run a fhort diftance, yet it would tire fooner than a horfe. He faid he would at all events try the experiment. He had heard the Wiandots fay, that I could run well, and now he would fee whether I could or not. I told him that I never had run all day, and of courfe was not accuftomed to that way of running. I never had run with the Wiandots more than feven or eight miles at one time. He faid that was nothing, we muft either catch thefe horfes or run all day.

In the morning early we left camp, and about funrife we ftarted after them, ftripped naked excepting breech-clouts and mockafons. About ten o'clock I loft fight of both Tontileaugo and the horfes, and did not fee them again until about three o'clock in the afternoon. As the horfes run all day, in about three or four miles fquare, at length they paffed where I was, and I fell in clofe after them. As I then had a long reft, I endeavored to keep ahead of Tontileaugo, and after fome time I could hear him after me calling *chakoh, chako-anaugh*, which fignifies, pull away or do your beft. We purfued on, and after fome time Tontileaugo paffed me, and about an hour before fundown, we defpaired of

6

catching thefe horfes and returned to camp where we had left our clothes.

I reminded Tontileaugo of what I had told him; he replied he did not know what horfes could do. They are wonderful ftrong to run; but withal we made them very tired. Tontileaugo then concluded, he would do as the Indians did with wild horfes, when out at war: which is to fhoot them through the neck under the mane, and above the bone, which will caufe them to fall and lie until they can halter them, and then they recover again. This he attempted to do; but as the mare was very wild, he could not get fufficiently nigh to fhoot her in the proper place; however he fhot, the ball paffed too low, and killed her. As the horfe and colt ftayed at this place, we caught the horfe, and took him and the colt with us to camp.

We ftayed at this camp about two weeks, and killed a number of bears, racoons, and fome beavers. We made a canoe of elm bark, and Tontileaugo embarked in it. He arrived at the falls that night; whilft I, mounted on horfe back, with a bear fkin faddle, and bark ftirrups, proceeded by land to the falls: I came there the next morning, and we carried our canoe and loading paft the falls.

The river is very rapid for fome diftance above the falls, which are about twelve or fifteen feet nearly perpendicular. This river, called Canefadooharie, interlocks with the Weft branch of Mufkingum, runs nearly a north courfe, and empties into the fouth fide of Lake Erie, about eighty miles eaft from Sandufky, or betwixt Sandufky and Cayahaga.

On this laft route the land is nearly the fame, as that laft defcribed, only there is not fo much fwampy or wet ground.

We again proceeded towards the lake, I on horfe back, and Tontileaugo by water. Here the land is generally good, but I found fome difficulty in getting round fwamps and ponds. When we came to the lake I proceeded along the ftrand, and Tontileaugo near the fhore, fometimes paddling and fometimes polling his canoe along.

After fome time the wind arofe, and he went into the mouth of a fmall creek and encamped. Here we ftaid feveral days on account of high wind, which raifed the lake in great billows. While we were here Tontileaugo went out to hunt, and when he was gone a Wiandot came to our camp; I gave him a fhoulder of venifon which I had by the fire well roafted, and he received it gladly, told me he was hungry, and thanked me for my kindnefs. When Tontileaugo came home, I told him that a Wiandot had been at camp, and that I gave him a fhoulder of roafted venifon: he faid that was very well, and I fuppofe you gave him alfo fugar and bears oil, to eat with his venifon. I told him I did not; as the fugar and bears oil was down in the canoe I did not go for it. He replied you have behaved juft like a

Dutchman.* Do you not know that when ftrangers come to our camp, we ought always to give them the beft that we have? I acknowledged that I was wrong. He faid that he could excufe this, as I was but young; but I muft learn to behave like a warrior, and do great things, and never be found in any fuch little actions.

The lake being again calm,† we proceeded, and arrived fafe at Sunyendeand, which was a Wiandot town, that lay upon a fmall creek which empties into the Little Lake below the mouth of Sandufky.

The town was about eighty rood above the mouth of the creek, on the fouth fide of a large plain, on which timber grew, and nothing more but grafs or nettles. In fome places there were large flats, where nothing but grafs grew, about three feet high when grown, and in other places nothing but nettles, very rank, where the foil is extremely rich and loofe—here they planted corn. In this town there were alfo French traders, who pur-chafed our fkins and fur, and we all got new clothes, paint, tobacco, &c.

After I had got my new clothes, and my head done off like a red-headed wood-pecker, I, in company with a number of young Indians, went down to the corn field,

---

* The Dutch he called Skoharehaugo, which took its derivation from a Dutch fettlement called Skoharey.

† The lake when calm, appears to be of a fky blue colour; though when lifted in a veffel, it is like other clear water.

to fee the fquaws at work. When we came there, they afked me to take a hoe, which I did, and hoed for fome time. The fquaws applauded me as a good hand at the bufinefs; but when I returned to the town, the old men hearing of what I had done, chid me, and faid that I was adopted in the place of a great man, and muft not hoe corn like a fquaw. They never had occafion to reprove me for any thing like this again; as I never was extremely fond of work, I readily complied with their orders.

As the Indians on their return from the winter hunt, bring in with them large quantities of bears oil, fugar, dried venifon, &c., at this time they have plenty, and do not fpare eating or giving—thus they make way with their provifion as quick as poffible. They have no fuch thing as regular meals, breakfaft, dinner or fupper; but if any one, even the town folks, would go to the fame houfe, feveral times in one day, he would be invited to eat of the beft—and with them it is bad manners to refufe to eat when it is offered. If they will not eat it is interpreted as a fymptom of difpleafure, or that the perfons refufing to eat were angry with thofe who invited them.

At this time homony, plentifully mixed with bears oil and fugar; or dried venifon, bears oil and fugar, is what they offer to every one who comes in any time of the day; and fo they go on until their fugar, bear's oil and venifon is all gone, and then they have to eat homony by itſelf, without bread, ſalt, or any thing elſe; yet, ſtill they invite every one that comes in, to eat whilſt they have any thing to give. It is thought a ſhame, not to invite people to eat, while they have any thing; but, if they can in truth, only ſay we have got nothing to eat, this is accepted as an honorable apology. All the hunters and warriors continued in town about ſix weeks after we came in: they ſpent this time in painting, going from houſe to houſe, eating, ſmoking, and playing at a game reſembling dice, or huſtle-cap. They put a number of plumb-ſtones in a ſmall bowl; one ſide of each ſtone is black, and the other white; they then ſhake or huſtle the bowl, calling, *hits, hits, hits, honeſey, honeſey, rago, rago;* which ſignifies calling for white or black, or what they wiſh to turn up; they then turn the bowl, and count the whites and blacks. Some were beating their kind of drum, and ſinging; others were employed in playing on a ſort of flute, made of hollow cane; and others playing on the jewſ-harp. Some part of this time was alſo taken up in attending the council houſe, where the chiefs, and as many others as choſe, attended ; and at night they were frequently employed in ſinging and dancing. Towards the laſt of this time, which was in June, 1756, they were all en-gaged in preparing to go to war againſt the frontiers of Virginia: when they were equipped, they went through their ceremonies, ſung their war ſongs, &c. They all marched off, from fifteen to ſixty years of age; and fome boys only twelve years old, were equipped with their bows and arrows, and went to war; fo that none were left in town but fquaws and children, except my-felf, one very old man, and another about fifty years of age, who was lame.

The Indians were then in great hopes that they would drive all the Virginians over the lake, which is all the name they know for the fea. They had fome caufe for this hope, becaufe at this time, the Americans were alto-gether unacquainted with war of any kind, and confe-quently very unfit to ftand their hand with fuch fubtil enemies as the Indians were. The two old Indians afked me if I did not think that the Indians and French would fubdue all America, except New England, which they faid they had tried in old times. I told them I thought not: they faid they had already drove them all out of the mountains, and had chiefly laid wafte the great val-ley betwixt the North and South mountain, from Poto-mack to James River, which is a confiderable part of the beft land in Virginia, Maryland, and Pennfylvania, and that the white people appeared to them like fools; they could neither guard againft furprife, run, or fight. Thefe they faid were their reafons for faying that they would fubdue the whites. They afked me to offer my reafons for my opinion, and told me to fpeak my mind freely. I told them that the white people to the Eaft were very numerous, like the trees, and though they appeared to them to be fools, as they were not acquainted with their way of war, yet they were not fools; therefore after fome time they will learn your mode of war, and turn upon you, or at leaft defend themfelves. I found that the old men themfelves did not believe they could conquer America, yet they were willing to propagate the idea, in order to encourage the young men to go to war.

When the warriors left this town we had neither meat, fugar, or bears oil, left. All that we had then to live on was corn pounded into coarfe meal or fmall homony—this they boiled in water, which appeared like well-thickened foup, without falt or any thing elfe. For fome time, we had plenty of this kind of homony; at length we were brought to very fhort allowance, and as the warriors did not return as foon as they expected, we were in a ftarving condition, and but one gun in the town, and very little amunition. The old lame Wiandot concluded that he would go a hunting in a canoe, and take me with him, and try to kill deer in the water, as it was then watering time. We went up San-dufky a few miles, then turned up a creek and en-camped. We had lights prepared, as we were to hunt in the night, and alfo a piece of bark and fome bufhes fet up in the canoe, in order to conceal ourfelves from the deer. A little boy that was with us, held the light, I worked the canoe, and the old man, who had his gun loaded with large fhot, when we came near the deer, fired, and in this manner killed three deer, in part of one night. We went to our fire, ate heartily, and in the morning returned to town, in order to relieve the hungry and diftreffed.

When we came to town, the children were crying bitterly on account of pinching hunger. We delivered what we had taken, and though it was but little among fo many, it was divided according to the ftricteft rules of juftice. We immediately fet out for another hunt, but before we returned a part of the warriors had come in, and brought with them on horfe-back, a quantity of meat. Thefe warriors had divided into different parties, and all ftruck at different places in Augufta county. They brought in with them a confiderable number of fcalps, prifoners, horfes, and other plunder. One of the parties brought in with them, one Arthur Campbell, that is now Col. Campbell, who lives on Holfton River, near the Royal-Oak. As the Wiandots at Sunyendeand, and thofe at Detroit were connected, Mr. Campbell was taken to Detroit; but he remained fome time with me in this town : his company was very agreeable, and I was forry when he left me. During his ftay at Sunyendeand he borrowed my Bible, and made fome pertinent remarks on what he had read. One paffage was where it is faid, "It is good for a man that he bear the yoke in his youth." He faid we ought to be refigned to the will of Providence, as we were now bearing the yoke, in our youth. Mr. Campbell appeared to be then about fixteen or feventeen years of age.

7

There was a number of prifoners brought in by thefe parties, and when they were to run the gauntlet, I went and told them how they were to act. One John Savage was brought in, a middle-aged man, or about forty years old. He was to run the gauntlet. I told him what he had to do; and after this I fell into one of the ranks with the Indians, fhouting and yelling like them; and as they were not very fevere on him, as he paffed me, I hit him with a piece of pumpkin—which pleafed the Indians much, but hurt my feelings.

About the time that thefe warriors came in, the green corn was beginning to be of ufe; fo that we had either green corn or venifon, and fometimes both—which was comparatively high living. When we could have plenty of green corn, or roafting-ears, the hunters became lazy, and fpent their time as already mentioned, in finging and dancing &c. They appeared to be fulfilling the fcriptures beyond thofe who profefs to believe them, in that of taking no thought of to-morrow: and alfo in living in love, peace and friendfhip together, without difputes. In this refpect they fhame thofe who profefs Chriftianity.

In this manner we lived, until October, then the geefe, fwans, ducks, cranes, &c. came from the north, and alighted on this little Lake, without number or innumerable. Sunyendeand is a remarkable place for fifh, in the fpring, and fowl both in the fall and fpring.

As our hunters were now tired with indolence, and

fond of their own kind of exercife, they all turned out to fowling, and in this could fcarce mifs of fuccefs ; fo that we had now plenty of homony and the beft of fowls; and fometimes as a rarity we had a little bread, which was made of Indian corn meal, pounded in a homony-block, mixed with boiled beans, and baked in cakes under the afhes.

This, with us was called good living, though not equal to our fat, roafted and boiled venifon, when we went to the woods in the fall ; or bears meat and beaver in the winter; or fugar, bears oil, and dry venifon in the fpring.

Some time in October, another adopted brother, older than Tontileaugo, came to pay us a vifit at Sunyende-and, and he afked me to take a hunt with him on Cay-ahaga. As they always ufed me as a free man, and gave me the liberty of choofing, I told him that I was at-tached to Tontileaugo—had never feen him before, and therefore, afked fometime to confider of this. He told me that the party he was going with would not be along, or at the mouth of this little lake, in lefs than fix days, and I could in this time be acquainted with him, and judge for myfelf. I confulted with Tontileaugo on this occafion, and he told me that our old brother Tecaugh-retanego, (which was his name) was a chief, and a better man than he was ; and if I went with him I might ex-pect to be well ufed, but he faid I might do as I pleafed ; and if I ftaid he would ufe me as he had done. I told him that he had acted in every respect as a brother to me; yet I was much pleased with my old brother's conduct and conversation; and as he was going to a part of the country I had never been in, I wished to go with him—he said that he was perfectly willing.

I then went with Tecaughretanego to the mouth of the little lake, where he met with the company he intended going with, which was composed of Caughnewagas, and Ottawas. Here I was introduced to a Caughnewaga sister, and others I had never before seen. My sister's name was Mary, which they pronounced *Maully*. I asked Tecaughretanego how it came that she had an English name; he said that he did not know that it was an English name; but it was the name the priest gave her when she was baptized, which he said was the name of the mother of Jesus. He said there were a great many of the Caughnewagas and Wiandots, that were a kind of half Roman Catholics; but as for himself, he said, that the priest and him could not agree; as they held notions that contradicted both sense and reason, and had the assurance to tell him, that the book of God, taught them these foolish absurdities: but he could not believe the great and good spirit ever taught them any such nonsense: and therefore he concluded that the Indians' old religion was better than this new way of worshiping God.

The Ottawas have a very useful kind of tents which they carry with them, made of flags, plaited and stitched together in a very artful manner, fo as to turn rain, or wind well—each mat is made fifteen feet long and about five feet broad. In order to erect this kind of tent, they cut a number of long, ftraight poles, which they drive in the ground, in form of a circle, leaning inwards; then they fpread the matts on thefe poles—beginning at the bottom and extending up, leaving only a hole in the top uncovered—and this hole anfwers the place of a chimney. They make a fire of dry, fplit wood, in the middle, and fpread down bark mats and fkins for bedding, on which they fleep in a crooked pofture, all round the fire, as the length of their beds will not admit of ftretching themfelves. In place of a door they lift up one end of a mat and creep in, and let the mat fall down behind them.

Thefe tents are warm and dry, and tolerable clear of fmoke. Their lumber they keep under birch-bark canoes, which they carry out and turn up for a fhelter, where they keep every thing from the rain. Nothing is in the tents but themfelves and their bedding.

This company had four birch canoes and four tents. We were kindly received, and they gave us plenty of homony, and wild fowl, boiled and roafted. As the geefe, ducks, fwans, &c. here are well grain-fed, they were remarkably fat efpecially the green necked ducks.

The wild fowl here feed upon a kind of wild rice, that grows fpontaneoufly in the fhallow water, or wet places along the fides or in the corners of the lakes.

As the wind was high and we could not proceed on our voyage, we remained here feveral days, and killed abundance of wild fowl, and a number of racoons.

When a company of Indians are moving together on the lake, as it is at this time of the year often danger- ous failing, the old men hold a council; and when they agree to embark, every one is engaged immediately in making ready, without offering one word againft the meafure, though the lake may be boifterous and horrid. One morning tho' the wind appeared to me to be as high as in days paft, and the billows raging, yet the call was given *yohoh-yohoh*, which was quickly anfwered by all—*ooh-ooh* which fignifies agreed. We were all in- ftantly engaged in preparing to ftart, and had confider- able difficulties in embarking.

As foon as we got into our canoes we fell to paddling with all our might, making out from the fhore. Though thefe fort of canoes ride waves beyond what could be expected, yet the water feveral times dafhed into them. When we got out about half a mile from fhore, we hoifted fail, and as it was nearly a weft wind, we then feemed to ride the waves with eafe, and went on at a rapid rate. We then all laid down our paddles, except- ing one that fteered, and there was no water dafhed into our canoes, until we came near the fhore again. We failed about fixty miles that day, and encamped fome time before night.

The next day we again embarked and went on very

well for fome time; but the lake being boifterous, and
the wind not fair, we were obliged to make to fhore,
which we accomplifhed with hard work and fome difficulty in landing.—The next morning a council was held
by the old men.

As we had this day to pafs by a long precipice of
rocks, on the fhore about nine miles, which rendered it
impoffible for us to land, though the wind was high
and the lake rough; yet, as it was fair, we were all ordered to embark. We wrought ourfelves out from the
fhore and hoifted fail (what we ufed in place of fail
cloth, were our tent mats, which anfwered the place very
well) and went on for fome time with a fair wind, until
we were oppofite to the precipice, and then it turned
towards the fhore, and we began to fear we fhould be
caft upon the rocks. Two of the canoes were confiderably farther out from the rocks, than the canoe I was
in. Thofe who were fartheft out in the lake did not let
down their fails until they had paffed the precipice; but
as we were nearer the rock, we were obliged to lower
our fails, and paddle with all our might. With much
difficulty we cleared ourfelves of the rock and landed.
As the other canoes had landed before us, there were
immediately runners fent off to fee if we were all fafely
landed.

This night the wind fell, and the next morning the
lake was tolerably calm, and we embarked without difficulty, and paddled along near the fhore, until we came

to the mouth of Cayahaga, which empties into Lake Erie on the fouth fide, betwixt Canefadooharie and Prefq' Ifle.

We turned up Cayahaga and encamped—where we ftaid and hunted for feveral days; and fo we kept moving and hunting until we came to the forks of Cayahaga.

This is a very gentle river, and but few riffles, or fwift running places, from the mouth to the forks. Deer here were tolerably plenty, large, and fat; but bear and other game fcarce. The upland is hilly and principally fecond and third rate land. The timber chiefly black-oak, white-oak, hickory, dogwood, &c. The bottoms are rich and large, and the timber is walnut, locuft, mulberry, fugar-tree, red-haw, black-haw, wild-appletrees, &c. The Weft Branch of this river interlocks with the Eaft Branch of Mufkingum; and the Eaft Branch with the Big Beaver creek, that empties into the Ohio about thirty miles below Pittfburgh.

From the forks of Cayahaga to the Eaft Branch of Mufkingum, there is a carrying place, where the Indians carry their canoes &c. from the waters of Lake Erie, into the waters of the Ohio.

From the forks I went over with fome hunters, to the Eaft Branch of Mufkingum, where they killed feveral deer, a number of beavers, and returned heavy laden, with fkins and meat, which we carried on our backs, as we had no horfes.

The land here is chiefly fecond and third rate, and

the timber chiefly oak and hickory. A little above the forks, on the Eaft Branch of Cayahaga, are confiderable rapids, very rocky, for fome diftance; but no perpendicular falls.

About the firft of December, 1756, we were preparing for leaving the river: we buried our canoes, and as ufual hung up our fkins, and every one had a pack to carry: the fquaws alfo packed up their tents, which they carried in large rolls, that extended up above their heads; and though a great bulk, yet not heavy. We fteered about a fouth eaft courfe and could not march over ten miles per day. At night we lodged in our flag tents, which when erected, were nearly in the fhape of a fugar loaf, and about fifteen feet diameter at the ground.

In this manner we proceeded about forty miles, and wintered in thefe tents, on the waters of Beaver creek, near a little lake or large pond, which is about two miles long, and one broad, and a remarkable place for beaver.

It is a received opinion among the Indians, that the geefe turn to beavers and the fnakes to racoons; and though Tecaughretanego, who was a wife man, was not fully perfuaded that this was true; yet he feemed in fome meafure to be carried away with this whimfical notion. He faid that this pond had been always a plentiful place of beaver. Though he faid he knew them to be frequently all killed, (as he thought;) yet the next winter they would be as plenty as ever. And as the

8

beaver was an animal that did not travel by land, and there being no water communication, to, or from this pond—how could fuch a number of beavers get there year after year? But as this pond was alfo a confiderable place for geefe, when they came in the fall from the north, and alighted in this pond, they turned beavers, all but the feet, which remained nearly the fame.

I faid, that though there was no water communication, in, or out of this pond; yet it appeared that it was fed by fprings, as it was always clear and never ftagnated; and as a very large fpring rofe about a mile below this pond, it was likely that this fpring came from this pond. In the fall, when this fpring is comparatively low, there would be air under ground fufficient for the beavers to breathe in, with their heads above water, for they can not live long under water, and fo they might have a fubterraneous paffage by water into this pond.—Tecaughretanego, granted that it might be fo.

About the fides of this pond there grew great abundance of cranberries, which the Indians gathered up on the ice, when the pond was frozen over. Thefe berries were about as large as rifle bullets—of a bright red colour—an agreeable four, though rather too four of themfelves; but when mixed with fugar, had a very agreeable tafte.

In converfation with Tecaughretanego, I happened to be talking of the beavers' catching fifh. He afked me why I thought that the beaver caught fifh? I told him

that I had read of the beaver making dams for the con-
veniency of fifhing. He laughed, and made game of
me and my book. He faid the man that wrote that
book knew nothing about the beaver. The beaver
never did eat flefh of any kind; but lived on the bark
of trees, roots, and other vegetables.

In order to know certainly how this was, when we
killed a beaver I carefully examined the inteftines, but
found no appearance of fifh; I afterwards made an
experiment on a pet beaver which we had, and found
that it would neither eat fifh or flefh; therefore I acknowledged that the book I had read was wrong.

I afked him if the beaver was an amphibious animal,
or if it could live under water? He faid that the beaver
was a kind of fubterraneous water animal, that lives in
or near the water; but they were no more amphibious
than the ducks and geefe were—which was conftantly
proven to be the cafe, as all the beavers that are caught
in fteel traps are drowned, provided the trap be heavy
enough to keep them under water. As the beaver does
not eat fifh, I enquired of Tecaughretanego why the
beaver made fuch large dams? He faid they were of
ufe to them in various refpects—both for their fafety
and food. For their fafety, as by raifing the water over
the mouths of their holes, or fubterraneous lodging
places, they could not be eafily found: and as the
beaver feeds chiefly on the bark of trees, by raifing the
water over the banks, they can cut down fapplings for

bark to feed upon without going out much upon the land: and when they are obliged to go out on land for this food they frequently are caught by the wolves. As the beaver can run upon land, but little faſter than a water tortoiſe, and is no fighting animal, if they are any diſtance from the water they become an eaſy prey to their enemies.

I aſked Tecaughretanego, what was the uſe of the beaver's ſtones, or glands, to them;—as the ſhe beaver has two pair, which is commonly called the oil ſtones, and the bark ſtones? He ſaid that as the beavers are the dumbeſt of all animals, and ſcarcely ever make any noiſe; and as they were working creatures, they made uſe of this ſmell in order to work in concert. If an old beaver was to come on the bank and rub his breech upon the ground, and raiſe a perfume, the others will collect from different places and go to work: this is alſo of uſe to them in travelling, that they may thereby ſearch out and find their company. Cunning hunters finding this out, have made uſe of it againſt the beaver, in order to catch them. What is the bate which you ſee them make uſe of, but a compound of the oil and bark ſtones? By this perfume, which is only a falſe ſignal, they decoy them to the trap.

Near this pond, beaver was the principal game. Before the waters froze up, we caught a great many with wooden and ſteel traps: but after that, we hunted the beaver on the ice. Some places here the beavers build large houſes to live in; and in other places they have ſubterraneous lodgings in the banks. Where they lodge in the ground we have no chance of hunting them on the ice; but where they have houſes we go with malls and handſpikes, and break all the hollow ice, to prevent them from getting their heads above the water under it. Then we break a hole in the houſe and they make their eſcape into the water; but as they cannot live long under water, they are obliged to go to ſome of thoſe broken places to breathe, and the Indians commonly put in their hands, catch them by the hind leg, haul them on the ice and tomahawk them. Sometimes they ſhoot them in the head, when they raiſe it above the water. I aſked the Indians if they were not afraid to catch the beavers with their hands? they ſaid no: they were not much of a biting crea- ture; yet if they would catch them by the fore foot they would bite.

I went out with Tecaughretanego, and ſome others a beaver hunting: but we did not ſucceed, and on our return we ſaw where ſeveral racoons had paſſed, while the ſnow was ſoft; tho' there was now a cruſt upon it, we all made a halt looking at the racoon tracks. As they ſaw a tree with a hole in it they told me to go and ſee if they had gone in thereat; and if they had to hal- loo, and they would come and take them out. When I went to that tree I found they had gone paſt; but I ſaw another the way they had went, and proceeded to

examine that, and found they had gone up it. I then
began to holloo, but could have no anfwer.

As it began to fnow and blow moft violently, I returned and proceeded after my company, and for fome
time could fee their tracks; but the old snow being
only about three inches deep, and a cruft upon it, the
prefent driving fnow foon filled up the tracks. As I
had only a bow, arrows, and tomahawk, with me, and
no way to ftrike fire, I appeared to be in a difmal fituation—and as the air was dark with fnow, I had little
more profpeçt of fteering my courfe, than I would in
the night. At length I came to a hollow tree, with a
hole at one fide that I could go in at. I went in, and
found that it was a dry place, and the hollow about
three feet diameter, and high enough for me to ftand in.
I found that there was alfo a confiderable quantity of
foft, dry rotten wood, around this hollow: I therefore
concluded that I would lodge here; and that I would
go to work, and ftop up the door of my houfe. I
ftripped off my blanket, (which was all the clothes that
I had, excepting a breech-clout, leggins, and mockafons,) and with my tomahawk, fell to chopping at the
top of a fallen tree that lay near and carried wood and
fet it up on end againft the door, until I had it three
or four feet thick, all round, excepting a hole I had left
to creep in at. I had a block prepared that I could
haul after me, to ftop this hole: and before I went in I
put in a number of fmall fticks, that I might more

effectually ftop it on the infide. When I went in, I took my tomahawk and cut down all the dry, rotten wood I could get, and beat it fmall. With it I made a bed like a goofe-neft or hog-bed, and with the fmall fticks ftopped every hole, until my houfe was almoft dark. I ftripped off my mockafons, and danced in the centre of my bed for about half an hour, in order to warm myfelf. In this time my feet and whole body were agreeably warmed. The fnow, in the mean while, had ftopped all the holes, fo that my houfe was as dark as a dungeon; though I knew it could not yet be dark out of doors. I then coiled myfelf up in my blanket, lay down in my little round bed, and had a tolerable nights lodging. When I awoke, all was dark—not the leaft glimmering of light was to be feen. Immediately I recollected that I was not to expect light in this new habitation, as there was neither door nor window in it. As I could hear the ftorm raging, and did not fuffer much cold, as I was then fituated, I concluded I would ftay in my neft until I was certain it was day. When I had reafon to conclude that it furely was day, I arofe and put on my mockafons, which I had laid under my head to keep from Freezing. I then endeavored to find the door, and had to do all by the fenfe of feeling, which took me fome time. At length I found the block, but it being heavy, and a large quantity of fnow having fallen on it, at the firft attempt I did not move it. I then felt terrified—among all the hardfhips I had fuftained, I never knew before, what it was to be thus deprived of light. This, with the other circumftances attending it, appeared grievous. I went ftraightway to bed again, wrapped my blanket round me, and lay and mufed awhile, and then prayed to Almighty God to direct and protect me, as he had done heretofore. I once again attempted to move away the block, which proved fuccefsful : it moved about nine inches. With this a confiderable quantity of fnow fell in from above, and I immediately received light ; fo that I found a very great fnow had fallen, above what I had ever feen in one night. I then knew why I could not eafily move the block, and I was fo rejoiced at obtaining the light, that all my other difficulties feemed to vanifh. I then turned into my cell, and returned God thanks for having once more received the light of Heaven. At length I belted my blanket about me, got my toma-hawk, bow and arrows, and went out of my den.

I was now in tolerable high fpirits, tho' the fnow had fallen above three feet deep, in addition to what was on the ground before ; and the only imperfect guide I had, in order to fteer my courfe to camp, was the trees ; as the mofs generally grows on the north-weft fide of them, if they are ftraight. I proceeded on, wading through the fnow, and about twelve o'clock (as it appeared afterwards, from that time to night, for it was yet cloudy,) I came upon the creek that our camp was on, about half a mile below the camp ; and when I came in fight of the camp, I found that there was great joy, by the fhouts and yelling of the boys, &c.

When I arrived, they all came round me, and received me gladly; but at this time no queftions were afked, and I was taken into a tent, where they gave me plenty of fat beaver meat, and then afked me to fmoke. When I had done, Tecaughretanego defired me to walk out to a fire they had made. I went out, and they all collected round me, both men, women, and boys. Tecaughretanego afked me to give them a particular account of what had happened from the time they left me yefterday, until now. I told them the whole of the ftory, and they never interrupted me; but when I made a ftop, the intervals were filled with loud acclamations of joy. As I could not, at this time, talk Ottawa or Jibewa well, (which is nearly the fame) I delivered my ftory in Caughnewaga. As my fifter Molly's hufband was a Jibewa and could underftand Caughnewaga, he acted as interpreter, and delivered my ftory to the Jibewas and Ottawas, which they received with pleafure. When all this was done, Tecaughretanego made a fpeech to me in the following manner:

"*Brother*,

"You fee we have prepared fnow-fhoes to go after you, and were almoft ready to go, when you appeared; yet, as you had not been accuftomed to hardfhips in your country, to the eaft, we never expected to fee you alive. Now, we are glad to fee you, in various refpects;

9

we are glad to fee you on your own account; and we are glad to fee the profpect of your filling the place of a great man, in whofe room you were adopted. We do not blame you for what has happened, we blame ourfelves; becaufe, we did not think of this driving fnow filling up the tracks, until after we came to camp.

"*Brother,*

"Your conduct on this occafion hath pleafed us much: You have given us an evidence of your fortitude, fkill and refolution : and we hope you will always go on to do great actions, as it is only great actions that can make a great man."

I told my brother Tecaughretanego, that I thanked them for their care of me, and for the kindnefs I always received. I told him that I always wifhed to do great actions, and hoped I never would do any thing to dishonor any of thofe with whom I was connected. I likewife told my Jibewa brother-in-law to tell his people that I alfo thanked them for their care and kindnefs.

The next morning fome of the hunters went out on fnow-fhoes, killed feveral deer, and hauled fome of them into camp upon the fnow. They fixed their carrying ftrings, (which are broad in the middle, and fmall at each end,) in the fore feet and nofe of the deer, and laid the broad part of it on their heads or about their fhoulders, and pulled it along; and when it is moving, will not fink in the fnow much deeper than a fnow-fhoe; and when taken with the grain of the hair, flips along very eafy.

The fnow-fhoes are made like a hoop-net, and wrought with buck-fkin thongs. Each fhoe is about two feet and an half long, and about eighteen inches broad, before, and fmall behind, with crofs-bars, in order to fix or tie them to their feet. After the fnow had lay a few days, the Indians tomahawked the deer, by purfuing them in this manner.

About two weeks after this, there came a warm rain, and took away the chief part of the fnow, and broke up the ice; then we engaged in making wooden traps to catch beavers, as we had but few fteel traps. Thefe traps are made nearly in the fame manner as the racoon traps already defcribed.

One day as I was looking after my traps, I got benighted, by beaver ponds intercepting my way to camp; and as I had neglected to take fire-works with me, and the weather very cold, I could find no fuitable lodging-place, therefore the only expedient I could think of to keep myfelf from freezing, was exercife. I danced and halloo'd the whole night with all my might, and the next day came to camp. Though I fuffered much more this time than the other night I lay out, yet the Indians were not fo much concerned, as they thought I had fire-works with me; but when they knew how it was, they did not blame me. They faid that old hunters were frequently involved in this place, as the beaver dams were one above another on every creek and run, fo that it is hard to find a fording place. They applauded me for my fortitude, and faid as they had now plenty of beaver-fkins, they would purchafe me a new gun at Detroit, as we were to go there the next fpring; and then if I fhould chance to be loft in dark weather, I could make fire, kill provifion, and return to camp when the fun fhined. By being bewildered on the waters of Mufkingum, I loft repute, and was reduced to the bow and arrow; and by lying out two nights here, I regained my credit.

After fome time, the waters all froze again, and then, as formerly, we hunted beavers on the ice. Though beaver meat, without falt or bread, was the chief of our food this winter, yet we had always plenty, and I was well contented with my diet, as it appeared delicious fare, after the way we had lived the winter before.

Some time in February, we fcaffolded up our fur and fkins, and moved about ten miles in queft of a fugar camp or a fuitable place to make fugar, and encamped in a large bottom, on the head waters of Big Beaver creek. We had fome difficulty in moving, as we had a blind Caughnewaga boy about 15 years of age, to lead; and as this country is very brufhy, we frequently had him to carry;—We had alfo my Jibewa brother-in-law's father with us, who was thought by the Indians to be a great conjurer—his name was Manetohcoa—this old man was fo decrepit, that we had to carry him this route upon a bier,—and all our baggage to pack on our backs.

Shortly after we came to this place the fquaws began to make fugar. We had no large kettles with us this year, and they made the froft, in fome meafure, fupply the place of fire, in making fugar. Their large bark veffels, for holding the ftock-water, they made broad and fhallow; and as the weather is very cold here, it frequently freezes at night in fugar time; and the ice they break and caft out of the veffels. I afked them if they were not throwing away the fugar? they faid no; it was water they were cafting away, fugar did not freeze, and there was fcarcely any in that ice. They faid I might try the experiment, and boil fome of it, and fee what I would get. I never did try it; but I obferved that after feveral times freezing, the water that remained in the veffel, changed its colour and became brown and very fweet.

About the time we were done making fugar the fnow went off the ground; and one night a fquaw raifed an alarm. She faid fhe faw two men with guns in their hands, upon the bank on the other fide of the creek, fpying our tents—they were fuppofed to be John-fton's Mohawks. On this the fquaws were ordered to flip quietly out, fome diftance into the bufhes; and all who had either guns or bows were to fquat in the bufhes near the tents; and if the enemy rufhed up, we were to give them the firſt fire, and let the ſquaws have an opportunity of eſcaping. I got down beſide Tecaughretanego, and he whiſpered to me not to be afraid, for he would ſpeak to the Mohawks, and as they ſpake the ſame tongue that we did, they would not hurt the Caughnewagas, or me: but they would kill all the Jibewas and Ottawas that they could, and take us along with them. This news pleaſed me well, and I heartily wiſhed for the approach of the Mohawks.

Before we withdrew from the tents they had carried Manetohcoa to the fire, and gave him his conjuring tools; which were dyed feathers, the bone of the ſhoulder blade of the wild cat, tobacco, &c., and while we were in the buſhes, Manetohcoa was in a tent at the fire, conjuring away to the utmoſt of his ability. At length he called aloud for us all to come in, which was quickly obeyed. When we came in, he told us that after he had gone through the whole of his ceremony, and expeéted to ſee a number of Mohawks on the flat bone when it was warmed at the fire, the piétures of two wolves only appeared. He ſaid though there were no Mohawks about, we muſt not be angry with the ſquaw for giving a falſe alarm; as ſhe had occaſion to go out and happened to ſee the wolves, though it was moon light; yet ſhe got afraid, and ſhe conceited it was Indians, with guns in their hands, ſo he ſaid we might all go to ſleep, for there was no danger—and accordingly we did.

The next morning we went to the place, and found wolf tracks, and where they had fcratched with their feet like dogs; but there was no fign of mockafon tracks. If there is any fuch thing as a wizzard, I think Manetohcoa was as likely to be one as any man, as he was a profeffed worfhipper of the devil.—But let him be a conjuror or not, I am perfuaded that the Indians believed what he told them upon this occafion, as well as if it had come from an infallible oracle; or they would not, after fuch an alarm as this, go all to fleep in an unconcerned manner. This appeared to me the moft like witchcraft, of any thing I beheld while I was with them. Though I fcrutinized their proceedings in bufi-nefs of this kind, yet I generally found that their pre-tended witchcraft, was either art or miftaken notions, whereby they deceived themfelves.—Before a battle they fpy the enemy's motions carefully, and when they find that they can have confiderable advantage, and the great-eft profpect of fuccefs, then the old men pretend to con-jure, or to tell what the event will be,—and this they do in a figurative manner, which will bear fomething of a different interpretation, which generally comes to pafs nearly as they foretold; therefore the young warriors generally believed thefe old conjurors, which had a tendency to animate, and excite them to pufh on with vigor.

Some time in March 1757 we began to move back to the forks of Cayahaga, which was about forty or fifty miles; and as we had no horſes, we had all our baggage and ſeveral hundred weight of beaver ſkins, and ſome deer and bear ſkins—all to pack on our backs. The method we took to accompliſh this was by making ſhort days' journies. In the morning we would move on with as much as we were able to carry, about five miles, and encamp; and then run back for more. We commonly made three ſuch trips in the day. When we came to the great pond we ſtaid there one day to reſt ourſelves and to kill ducks and geeſe.

While we remained here I went in company with a young Caughnewaga, who was about fifteen or ſeventeen years of age, Chinnohete by name, in order to gather crannberries. As he was gathering berries at ſome diſtance from me, three Jibewa ſquaws crept up undiſcovered and made at him ſpeedily, but he nimbly eſcaped, and came to me apparently terrified. I aſked him what he was afraid of? he replied did you not ſee thoſe ſquaws? I told him I did, and they appeared to be in a very good humor. I aſked him wherefore then he was afraid of them? He ſaid the Jibewa ſquaws were very bad women, and had a very ugly cuſtom among them. I aſked him what that cuſtom was? he ſaid that when two or three of them could catch a young lad, that was betwixt a man and a boy, out by himſelf, if they could overpower him, they would ſtrip him by force in order to ſee whether he was coming on to be a man or not. He ſaid that was what they intended when they crawled up, and ran fo violently at him, but faid he, I am very glad that I fo narrowly efcaped. I then agreed with Chinnohete in condemning this as a bad cuftom, and an exceeding immodeft action for young women to be guilty of.

From our fugar camp on the head waters of Big Beaver creek, to this place is not hilly, and fome places the woods are tolerably clear: but in moft places exceed-ing brufhy. The land here is chiefly fecond and third rate. The timber on the upland is white-oak, black-oak, hickory and chefnut: there is alfo in fome places walnut up land, and plenty of good water. The bottoms here are generally large and good.

We again proceeded on from the pond to the forks of Cayahaga, at the rate of about five miles per day.

The land on this route is not very hilly, it is well watered, and in many places ill timbered, generally brufhy, and chiefly fecond and third rate land, inter-mixed with good bottoms.

When we came to the forks, we found that the fkins we had fcaffolded were all fafe. Though this was a public place, and Indians frequently paffing, and our fkins hanging up in view, yet there was none ftolen; and it is feldom that Indians do fteal anything from one another; and they fay they never did, until the white people came among them, and learned fome of them to lie, cheat and fteal,—but be that as it may, they never did curfe or fwear, until the whites learned them; fome

10

think their language will not admit of it, but I am not of that opinion; if I was fo difpofed, I could find language to curfe or fwear, in the Indian tongue.

I remember that Tecaughretanego, when fomething difpleafed him, faid, God damn it.—I afked him if he knew what he then faid? he faid he did; and mentioned one of their degrading expreffions, which he fuppofed to be the meaning or fomething like the meaning of what he had faid. I told him that it did not bear the leaft refemblance to it; that what he faid, was calling upon the great fpirit to punifh the object he was difpleafed with. He ftood for fometime amazed, and then faid, if this be the meaning of thefe words, what fort of people are the whites? when the traders were among us thefe words feemed to be intermixed with all their difcourfe. He told me to reconfider what I had faid, for he thought I muft be miftaken in my definition; if I was not miftaken, he said, the traders applied thefe words not only wickedly, but often times very foolifhly and contrary to fenfe or reafon. He faid he remembered once of a trader's accidentally breaking his gun lock, and on that occafion calling out aloud God damn it—furely faid he the gun lock was not an object worthy of punifhment for Owaneeyo, or the Great Spirit: he alfo obferved the traders often ufed this expreffion, when they were in a good humor and not difpleafed with anything.—I acknowledged that the traders ufed this expreffion very often, in a moft irrational, inconfiftent, and impious man-

ner; yet I ſtill aſſerted that I had given the true meaning of theſe words.—He replied, if ſo, the traders are
as bad as Oonaſahroona, or the under ground inhabitants, which is the name they give the devils; as they
entertain a notion that their place of reſidence is under
the earth.

We took up our birch-bark canoes which we had
buried, and found that they were not damaged by the
winter; but they not being ſufficient to carry all that
we now had, we made a large cheſnut bark canoe; as
elm bark was not to be found at this place.

We all embarked, and had a very agreeable paſſage
down the Cayahaga, and along the ſouth ſide of Lake
Erie, until we paſſed the mouth of Sanduſky; then the
wind aroſe, and we put in at the mouth of the Miami
of the Lake, at Cedar Point, where we remained ſeveral
days, and killed a number of Turkeys, geeſe, ducks and
ſwans. The wind being fair, and the lake not extremely
rough, we again embarked, hoiſted up ſails, and arrived
ſafe at the Wiandot town, nearly oppoſite to Fort Detroit, on the north ſide of the river. Here we found a
number of French traders, every one very willing to
deal with us for our beaver.

We bought ourſelves fine clothes, amunition, paint,
tobacco, &c. and according to promiſe, they purchaſed
me a new gun: yet we had parted with only about one-
third of our beaver. At length a trader came to town
with French Brandy: We purchaſed a keg of it, and

held a council about who was to get drunk, and who was to keep fober. I was invited to get drunk, but I refufed the propofal—then they told me that I muſt be one of thoſe who were to take care of the drunken people. I did not like this; but of two evils I choſe that which I thought was the leaſt—and fell in with thoſe who were to conceal the arms, and keep every dangerous weapon we could, out of their way, and endeavor, if poſſible to keep the drinking club from killing each other, which was a very hard taſk. Several times we hazarded our own lives, and got ourſelves hurt, in preventing them from flaying each other. Before they had finiſhed this keg, near one-third of the town was introduced to this drinking club; they could not pay their part, as they had already difpoſed of all their ſkins; but that made no odds, all were welcome to drink.

When they were done with this keg, they applied to the traders, and procured a kettle full of brandy at a time, which they divided out with a large wooden fpoon,—and ſo they went on and never quit while they had a ſingle beaver ſkin.

When the trader had got all our beaver, he moved off to the Ottawa town, about a mile above the Wiandot town.

When the brandy was gone, and the drinking club fober, they appeared much dejeᴄted. Some of them were crippled, others badly wounded, a number of their fine new ſhirts tore, and ſeveral blankets were burned:—

a number of fquaws were alfo in this club, and neglected their corn planting.

We could now hear the effects of the brandy in the Ottawa town. They were finging and yelling in the moft hideous manner, both night and day; but their frolic ended worfe than ours; five Ottawas were killed and a great many wounded.

After this a number of young Indians were getting their ears cut, and they urged me to have mine cut like-wife; but they did not attempt to compel me, though they endeavored to perfuade me. The principal argu-ments they ufed were its being a very great ornament, and alfo the common fafhion—The former I did not believe, and the latter I could not deny. The way they performed this operation was by cutting the flefhy part of the circle of the ear clofe to the griftle quite through. When this was done they wrapt rags round this flefhy part until it was entirely healed; then they hung lead to it and ftretched it to a wonderful length: when it was sufficiently ftretched, they wrapt the flefhy part round with brafs wire, which formed it into a femicircle about four inches diameter.

Many of the young men were now exercifing them-felves in a game refembling foot ball; though they com-monly ftruck the ball with a crooked ftick, made for that purpofe; alfo a game fomething like this, wherein they ufed a wooden ball, about three inches diameter, and the inftrument they moved it with was a ftrong ftaff about five feet long, with a hoop net on the end of it, large enough to contain the ball. Before they begin the play, they lay off about half a mile diftance in a clear plain, and the oppofite parties all attend at the centre, where a difinterefted perfon cafts up the ball then the opofite parties all contend for it. If any one gets it into his net, he runs with it the way he wifhes it to go, and they all purfue him. If one of the oppofite party overtakes the perfon with the ball, he gives the ftaff a ftroke which caufes the ball to fly out of the net; then they have another debate for it; and if the one that gets it can outrun all the oppofite party, and can carry it quite out, or over the line at the end, the game is won; but this feldom happens. When any one is running away with the ball, and is like to be overtaken, he commonly throws it, and with this inftrument can caft it fifty or fixty yards. Sometimes when the ball is almoft at the one end, matters will take a fudden turn, and the oppofite party may quickly carry it out at the other end. Oftentimes they will work a long while back and forward before they can get the ball over the line, or win the game.

About the firft of June, 1757, the warriors were preparing to go to war, in the Wiandot, Pottowatomy, and Ottawa towns; alfo a great many Jibewas came down from the upper lakes; and after finging their war fongs and going through their common ceremonies, they marched off againft the frontiers of Virginia, Maryland

and Pennſylvania, in their uſual manner, ſinging the travelling ſong, ſlow firing, &c.

On the north ſide of the river St. Laurence, oppoſite to Fort Detroit, there is an iſland, which the Indians call the Long Iſland, and which they ſay is above one thouſand miles long, and in ſome places above one hundred miles broad. They further ſay that the great river that comes down by Caneſatauga and that empties into the main branch of St. Laurence, above Montreal, originates from one ſource, with the St. Lawrence, and forms this iſland.

Oppoſite to Detroit, and below it, was originally a prairie, and laid off in lots about ſixty rods broad, and a great length: each lot is divided into two fields, which they cultivate year about. The principal grain that the French raiſed in theſe fields was ſpring wheat and peas.

They built all their houſes on the front of theſe lots on the river ſide; and as the banks of the river are very low, ſome of the houſes are not above three or four feet above the ſurface of the water; yet they are in no danger of being diſturbed by freſhes, as the river ſeldom riſes above eighteen inches; becauſe it is the communication, of the river St. Laurence, from one lake to another.

As dwelling-houſes, barns, and ſtables are all built on the front of theſe lots; at a diſtance it appears like a continued row of houſes in a town, on each ſide of the river for a long way. Theſe villages, the town, the river and the plains, being all in view at once, affords a moſt delightful profpeƈt.

The inhabitants here chiefly drink the river water; and as it comes from the northward it is very wholeſome.

The land here is principally ſecond rate, and comparatively ſpeaking, a ſmall part is firſt or third rate; tho about four or five miles ſouth of Detroit, there is a ſmall portion that is worſe than what I would call third rate, which produces abundance of hurtle berries.

There is plenty of good meadow ground here, and a great many marſhes that are overſpread with water.— The timber is elm, ſugar-tree, black-aſh, white-aſh, abundance of water-aſh, oak, hickory, and ſome walnut.

About the middle of June the Indians were almoſt all gone to war, from ſixteen to ſixty; yet Tecaughretanego remained in town with me. Tho he had formerly, when they were at war with the ſouthern nations been a great warrior, and an eminent counſellor; and I think as clear and as able a reaſoner upon any ſubjeƈt that he had an opportunity of being acquainted with, as I ever knew; yet he had all along been againſt this war, and had ſtrenuouſly oppoſed it in council. He ſaid if the Engliſh and French had a quarrel let them fight their own battles themſelves; it is not our buſineſs to intermeddle therewith.

Before the warriors returned we were very ſcarce of proviſion: and tho we did not commonly ſteal from one another; yet we ftole during this time any thing that we could eat from the French, under the notion that it was juft for us to do fo; becaufe they fupported their foldiers; and our fquaws, old men and children were fuffering on the account of the war, as our hunters were all gone.

Some time in Auguft the warriors returned, and brought in with them a great many fcalps, prifoners, horfes and plunder; and the common report among the young warriors, was, that they would intirely fubdue Tulhafaga, that is the Englifh, or it might be literally rendered the Morning Light inhabitants.

About the firft of November a number of families were preparing to go on their winter hunt, and all agreed to crofs the lake together. We encamped at the mouth of the river the firft night, and a council was held, whether we would crofs thro' by the three iflands, or coaft it round the lake. Thefe iflands lie in a line acrofs the lake, and are juft in fight of each other. Some of the Wiandots or Ottawas frequently make their winter hunt on thefe iflands. Tho excepting wild fowl and fifh, there is fcarcely any game here but racoons which are amazingly plenty, and exceeding large and fat; as they feed upon the wild rice, which grows in abundance in wet places round thefe iflands. It is faid that each hunter in one winter will catch one thoufand racoons.

It is a received opinion among the Indians that the

fnakes and racoons are tranfmutable; and that a great many of the fnakes turn racoons every fall, and racoons fnakes every fpring. This notion is founded on obfervations made on the fnakes and racoons in this ifland.

As the racoons here lodge in rocks, the trappers make their wooden traps at the mouth of the holes; and as they go daily to look at their traps, in the winter feafon, they commonly find them filled with racoons; but in the fpring or when the froft is out of the ground they fay, they then find their traps filled with large rattle fnakes. And therefore conclude that the racoons are transformed. They alfo fay that the reafon why they are fo remarkably plenty in the winter, is, every fall the fnakes turn racoons again.

I told them that tho I had never landed on any of thefe iflands, yet from the unanimous accounts I had received, I believed that both fnakes and racoons were plenty there; but no doubt they all remained there both fummer and winter, only the fnakes were not to be feen in the latter; yet I did not believe they were tranfmutable.

Thefe iflands are but feldom vifited; becaufe early in the fpring and late in the fall it is dangerous failing in their bark canoes; and in the fummer they are fo infefted with various kinds of ferpents, (but chiefly rattle fnakes,) that it is dangerous landing.

I fhall now quit this digreffion, and return to the refult of the council at the mouth of the river. We concluded to coaft it round the lake, and in two days we came to the mouth of the Miami of the Lake, and landed on cedar point, where we remained feveral days. Here we held a council, and concluded we would take a driving hunt in concert, and in partnerfhip.

The river in this place is about a mile broad, and as it and the lake forms a kind of neck, which terminates in a point, all the hunters (which were fifty-three) went up the river, and we fcattered ourfelves from the river to the lake. When we firft began to move we were not in fight of each other, but as we all raifed the yell, we could move regularly together by the noife. At length we came in fight of each other and appeared to be marching in good order; before we came to the point, both the fquaws and boys in the canoes were fcattered up the river, and along the lake, to prevent the deer from making their efcape by water. As we advanced near the point the guns began to crack flowly; and after fome time the firing was like a little engagement. The fquaws and boys were bufy tomahawking the deer in the water, and we fhooting them down on the land:—We killed in all about thirty deer; tho a great many made their efcape by water.

We had now great feafting and rejoicing, as we had plenty of homony, venifon, and wild fowl. The geefe at this time appeared to be preparing to move fouthward— It might be afked what is meant by the geefe preparing to move? The Indians reprefent them as holding a great council at this time concerning the weather in order to conclude upon a day, that they may all at or near one time leave the Northern Lakes, and wing their way to the fouthern bays. When matters are brought to a conclufion and the time appointed that they are to take wing, then they fay, a great number of expreffes are fent off, in order to let the different tribes know the refult of this council, that they may be all in readinefs to move at the time appointed. As there is a great commotion among the geefe at this time, it would appear by their actions, that fuch a council had been held. Certain it is, that they are led by inftinct to act in concert and to move off regularly after their leaders.

Here our company feparated. The chief part of them went up the Miami river, that empties into Lake Erie, at cedar point, whilft we proceeded on our journey in company with Tecaughretanego, Tontileaugo, and two families of the Wiandots.

As cold weather was now approaching, we began to feel the doleful effects of extravagantly and foolifhly fpending the large quantity of beaver we had taken in our laft winter's hunt. We were all nearly in the fame circumftances—fcarcely one had a fhirt to his back; but each of us had an old blanket which we belted round us in the day, and flept in at night, with a deer or bear fkin under us for our bed.

When we came to the falls of Sandufky, we buried our birch bark canoes as ufual, at a large burying place

for that purpofe, a little below the falls. At this place
the river falls about eight feet over a rock, but not perpendicular. With much difficulty we pufhed up our
wooden canoes, fome of us went up the river, and the
reft by land with the horfes, until we came to the great
meadows or prairies that lie between Sandufky and
Sciota.

When we came to this place we met with fome Ottawa
hunters, and agreed with them to take, what they call a
ring hunt, in partnerfhip. We waited until we expected
rain was near falling to extinguifh the fire, and then we
kindled a large circle in the prairie. At this time, or
before the bucks began to run a great number of deer
lay concealed in the grafs, in the day, and moved about
in the night; but as the fire burned in towards the centre of the circle, the deer fled before the fire: the Indians
were fcattered alfo at fome diftance before the fire, and
fhot them down every opportunity, which was very frequent, efpecially as the circle became fmall. When we
came to divide the deer, there were above ten to each
hunter, which were all killed in a few hours. The rain
did not come on that night to put out the out-fide circle of the fire, and as the wind arofe, it extended thro
the whole prairie, which was about fifty miles in length,
and in fome places near twenty in breadth. This put
an end to our ring hunting this feafon, and was in other
refpects an injury to us in the hunting bufinefs; fo that
upon the whole we received more harm than benefit by

our rapid hunting frolic. We then moved from the north end of the glades, and encamped at the carrying place.

This place is in the plains betwixt a creek that empties into Sanduſky, and one that runs into Sciota: and at the time of high water, or in the ſpring ſeaſon, there is but about one half mile of portage, and that very level, and clear of rocks, timber or ſtones; ſo that with a little digging there may be water carriage the whole way from Sciota to Lake Erie.

From the mouth of Sanduſky to the falls is chiefly firſt rate land, lying flat or level, intermixed with large bodies of clear meadows, where the graſs is exceeding rank, and in many places three or four feet high. The timber is oak, hickory, walnut, cherry, black-aſh, elm, ſugar-tree, buckeye, locuſt and beech. In ſome places there is wet timber land—the timber in theſe places is chiefly water-aſh, ſycamore, or button-wood.

From the falls to the prairies, the land lies well to the ſun, it is neither too flat nor too hilly—and chiefly firſt rate. The timber nearly the ſame as below the falls, excepting the water-aſh.—There is alſo here, ſome plats of beech land, that appears to be ſecond rate, as it frequently produces ſpice-wood. The prairie appears to be a tolerable fertile ſoil, tho in many places too wet for cultivation; yet I apprehend it would produce timber, were it only kept from fire.

The Indians are of the opinion that the ſquirrels

plant all the timber; as they bury a number of nuts for food, and only one at a place. When a fquirrel is killed the various kinds of nuts thus buried will grow.

I have obferved that when thefe prairies have only efcaped fire for one year, near where a fingle tree ftood, there was a young growth of timber fuppofed to be planted by the fquirrels; but when the prairies were again burned, all this young growth was immediately confumed; as the fire rages in the grafs, to fuch a pitch, that numbers of racoons are thereby burned to death.

On the weft fide of the prairie, or betwixt that and Sciota, there is a large body of firft rate land—the timber, walnut, locuft, fugar-tree, buckeye, cherry, afh, elm, mulberry, plumb trees, fpicewood, black-haw, red-haw, oak and hickory.

About the time the bucks quit running, Tontileaugo his wife and children, Tecaughrctanego, his fon Nungany and myfelf left the Wiandot camps at the carrying place, and croffed the Sciota river at the fouth end of the glades, and proceeded on about a fouth-weft courfe to a large creek called Ollentangy, which I believe interlocks with the waters of the Miami, and empties into Sciota on the weft fide thereof. From the fouth end of the prairie to Ollentangy, there is a large quantity of beech land, intermixed with firft rate land. Here we made our winter hut, and had confiderable fuccefs in hunting.

After fome time one of Tontileaugo's ftep-fons, a)

lad about eight years of age) offended him, and he gave the boy a moderate whipping, which much difpleafed his Wiandot wife. She acknowledged that the boy was guilty of a fault, but thought that he ought to have been ducked, which is their ufual mode of chaftifement. She faid fhe could not bear to have her fon whipped like a fervant or flave—and fhe was fo difpleafed that when Tontileaugo went out to hunt, fhe got her two horfes, and all her effects, (as in this country the hufband and wife have feparate interefts) and moved back to the Wiandot camps that we had left.

When Tontileaugo returned, he was much difturbed on hearing of his wife's elopement, and faid that he would never go after her were it not that he was afraid that fhe would get bewildered, and that his children that fhe had taken with her, might fuffer. Tontileaugo went after his wife, and when they met they made up the quarrel, and he never returned ; but left Tecaughretanego and his fon, (a boy about ten years of age) and myfelf, who remained here in our hut all winter.

Tecaughretanego who had been a firft rate warior, ftatefman and hunter; and though he was now near fixty years of age, he was yet equal to the common run of hunters, but fubject to the rheumatifm, which deprived him of the ufe of his legs.

Shortly after Tontileaugo left us, Tecaughretanego became lame, and could fcarcely walk out of our hut for two months. I had confiderable fuccefs in hunting and trapping. Though Tecaughretanego endured much pain and mifery, yet he bore it all with wonderful patience, and would often endeavor to entertain me with chearful converfation. Sometimes he would applaud me for my diligence, fkill and activity—and at other times he would take great care in giving me inftructions concerning the hunting and trapping bufinefs. He would alfo tell me that if I failed of fuccefs, we would fuffer very much, as we were about forty miles from any one living, that we knew of; yet he would not intimate that he apprehended we were in any danger, but ftill fuppofed that I was fully adequate to the tafk.

Tontileaugo left us a little before Chriftmas, and from that until fome time in February, we had always plenty of bear meat, venifon, &c. During this time I killed much more than we could ufe, but having no horfes to carry in what I killed, I left part of it in the woods. In February there came a fnow, with a cruft, which made a great noife when walking on it, and frightened away the deer; and as bear and beaver were fcarce here, we got entirely out of provifion. After I had hunted two days without eating any thing, and had very fhort allowance for fome days before, I returned late in the evening faint and weary. When I came into our hut, Tecaughretanego afked what fuccefs? I told him not any. He afked me if I was not very hungry? I replied that the keen appetite feemed to be in fome meafure removed, but I was both faint and weary. He commanded Nunganey his little fon, to bring me fomething to eat, and he brought me a kettle with fome bones and broth,—after eating a few mouthfuls my appetite violently returned, and I thought the victuals had a moft agreeable realifh, though it was only fox and wildcat bones, which lay about the camp, which the ravens and turkey-buzzards had picked—thefe Nunganey had collected and boiled, until the finews that remained on the bones would ftrip off. I fpeedily finifhed my allowance, fuch as it was, and when I had ended my *sweet* repaft, Tecaughretanego afked me how I felt? I told him that I was much refrefhed. He then handed me his pipe and pouch, and told me to take a fmoke. I did fo. He then faid he had fomething of importance to tell me, if I was now compofed and ready to hear it. I told him that I was ready to hear him. He faid the reafon why he deferred his fpeech till now, was becaufe few men are in a right humor to hear good talk, when they are extremely hungry, as they are then generally fretful and difcompofed; but as you appear now to enjoy calmnefs and ferenity of mind, I will now communicate to you the thoughts of my heart, and thofe things that I know to be true.

" *Brother*,

" As you have lived with the white people, you have not had the fame advantage of knowing that the great being above feeds his people, and gives them their meat in due feafon, as we Indians have, who are frequently out of provifions, and yet are wonderfully fupplied, and that fo frequently that it is evidently the hand of the great Owaneeyo* that doth this: whereas the white people have commonly large ftocks of tame cattle, that they can kill when they pleafe, and alfo their barns and cribs filled with grain, and therefore have not the fame opportunity of feeing and knowing that they are fupported by the ruler of Heaven and Earth.

"*Brother,*

"I know that you are now afraid that we will all perifh with hunger, but you have no juft reafon to fear this.

"*Brother,*

"I have been young, but am now old—I have been frequently under the like circumftance that we now are, and that fome time or other in almoft every year of my life; yet, I have hitherto been fupported, and my wants fupplied in time of need.

"*Brother,*

"Owaneeyo fome times fuffers us to be in want, in order to teach us our dependance upon him, and to let us know that we are to love and ferve him: and like-wife to know the worth of the favors that we receive, and to make us more thankful.

---

* This is the name of God, in their tongue, and fignifies the owner and ruler of all things.

" *Brother,*

" Be affured that you will be fupplied with food, and that juft in the right time; but you muft continue diligent in the ufe of means—go to fleep, and rife early in the morning and go a hunting—be ftrong and exert yourfelf like a man, and the great fpirit will direct your way."

The next morning I went out, and fteered about an eaft courfe. I proceeded on flowly for about five miles, and faw deer frequently, but as the cruft on the fnow made a great noife, they were always running before I fpied them, fo that I could not get a fhoot. A violent appetite returned, and I became intolerably hungry;— it was now that I concluded I would run off to Pennfylvania, my native country. As the fnow was on the ground, and Indian hunters almoft the whole of the way before me, I had but a poor profpect of making my efcape; but my cafe appeared defperate. If I ftaid here I thought I would perifh with hunger, and if I met with Indians, they could but kill me.

I then proceeded on as faft as I could walk, and when I got about ten or twelve miles from our hut, I came upon frefh buffaloe tracks,—I purfued after, and in a fhort time came in fight of them, as they were paffing through a fmall glade—I ran with all my might, and headed them, where I lay in ambufh, and killed a very large cow. I immediately kindled a fire and began to roaft meat, but could not wait till it was done—I ate it almoſt raw. When hunger was abated I began to be tenderly concerned for my old Indian brother, and the little boy I had left in a periſhing condition. I made haſte and packed up what meat I could carry, ſecured what I left from the wolves, and returned homewards.

I ſcarcely thought on the old man's ſpeech while I was almoſt diſtracted with hunger, but on my return was much affected with it, reflected on myſelf for my hard-heartedneſs and ingratitude, in attempting to run off and leave the venerable old man and little boy to periſh with hunger. I alſo conſidered how remarkably the old man's ſpeech had been verified in our providentially obtaining a ſupply. I thought alſo of that part of his ſpeech which treated of the fractious diſpoſitions of hungry people, which was the only excuſe I had for my baſe inhumanity, in attempting to leave them in the moſt deplorable ſituation.

As it was moon-light, I got home to our hut, and found the old man in his uſual good humor. He thanked me for my exertion, and bid me ſit down, as I muſt certainly be fatigued, and he commanded Nunganey to make haſte and cook. I told him I would cook for him, and let the boy lay ſome meat on the coals, for himſelf—which he did, but ate it almoſt raw, as I had done. I immediately hung on the kettle with ſome water, and cut the beef in thin ſlices, and put them in: —when it had boiled awhile, I propoſed taking it off the fire, but the old man replied, "let it be done enough." This he faid in as patient and unconcerned a manner, as if he had not wanted one fingle meal. He commanded Nunganey to eat no more beef at that time, leaft he might hurt himfelf; but told him to fit down, and after fome time he might fup fome broth—this command he reluctantly obeyed.

When we were all refrefhed, Tecaughretanego delivered a fpeech upon the neceffity and pleafure of receiving the neceffary fupports of life with thankfulnefs, knowing that Owaneeyo is the great giver. Such fpeeches from an Indian, may be tho't by thofe who are unacquainted with them, altogether incredible; but when we reflect on the Indian war, we may readily conclude that they are not an ignorant or ftupid fort of people, or they would not have been fuch fatal enemies. When they came into our country they outwitted us—and when we fent armies into their country, they outgeneralled, and beat us with inferior force. Let us alfo take into confideration that Tecaughretanego was no common perfon, but was among the Indians, as Socrates in the ancient Heathen world; and it may be, equal to him—if not in wifdom and learning, yet, perhaps in patience and fortitude. Notwithftanding Tecaughretanego's uncommon natural abilities, yet in the fequel of this hiftory you will fee the deficiency of the light of nature, unaided by revelation, in this truly great man.

The next morning Tecaughretanego defired me to go back and bring another load of buffaloe beef: As I proceeded to do fo, about five miles from our hut I found a bear tree. As a fapling, grew near the tree, and reached near the hole that the bear went in at, I got dry dozed or rotten wood, that would catch and hold fire almoft as well as fpunk. This wood I tied up in bunches, fixed them on my back, and then climbed up the fapling, and with a pole, I put them touched with fire, into the hole, and then came down and took my gun in my hand. After fome time the bear came out, and I killed and fkinned it, packed up a load of the meat, (after fecuring the remainder from the wolves) and returned home before night. On my return my old brother and his fon were much rejoiced at my fuc-cefs. After this we had plenty of provifion.

We remained here until fome time in April 1758. At this time Tecaughretanego had recovered fo, that he could walk about. We made a bark canoe, embarked, and went down Ollentangy fome diftance, but the water being low, we were in danger of fplitting our canoe upon the rocks: therefore Tecaughretanego concluded we would encamp on fhore, and pray for rain.

When we encamped, Tecaughretanego made himfelf a fweat-houfe; which he did by fticking a number of hoops in the ground, each hoop forming a femi-circle— this he covered all round with blankets and fkins; he then prepared hot ftones, which he rolled into this hut, and then went into it himfelf, with a little kettle of water in his hand, mixed with a variety of herbs, which he had formerly cured, and had now with him in his pack—they afforded an odoriferous perfume. When he was in, he told me to pull down the blankets behind him, and cover all up cloſe, which I did, and then he began to pour water upon the hot ſtones, and to ſing aloud. He continued in this vehement hot place about fifteen minutes:—all this he did in order to purify him-ſelf before he would addreſs the Supreme Being. When he came out of his ſweat-houſe, he began to burn to-bacco and to pray. He began each petition with *oh, ho, ho, ho,* which is a kind of aſpiration, and ſignifies an ardent wiſh. I obſerved that all his petitions were only for immediate, or preſent temporal bleſſings. He began his addreſs by thankſgiving, in the following manner:

"O great being! I thank thee that I have obtained the uſe of my legs again—that I am now able to walk about and kill turkeys, &c. without feeling exquiſite pain and miſery: I know that thou art a hearer and a helper, and therefore I will call upon thee.

"*Oh, ho, ho, ho,*

"Grant that my knees and ancles may be right well, and that I may be able, not only to walk, but to run, and to jump logs, as I did laſt fall.

"*Oh, ho, ho, ho,*

"Grant that on this voyage we may frequently kill bears, as they may be croſſing the Sciota and San-duſky.

"*Oh, ho, ho, ho,*

"Grant that we may kill plenty of Turkeys along the banks, to ftew with our fat bear meat.

"*Oh, ho, ho, ho,*

"Grant that rain may come to raife the Ollentangy about two or three feet, that we may crofs in fafety down to Sciota, without danger of our canoe being wrecked on the rocks;—and now, O great being! thou knoweft how matters ftand—thou knoweft that I am a great lover of tobacco, and though I know not when I may get any more, I now make a prefent of the laft I have unto thee, as a free burnt offering; therefore I expect thou wilt hear and grant thefe requefts, and I thy fervant will return thee thanks, and love thee for thy gifts."

During the whole of this fcene I fat by Tecaughretanego, and as he went through it with the greateft folemnity, I was ferioufly affected with his prayers. I remained duly compofed until he came to the burning of the tobacco, and as I knew that he was a great lover of it, and faw him caft the laft of it into the fire, it excited in me a kind of meriment, and I infenfibly fmiled. Tecaughretanego obferved me laughing, which difpleafed him, and occafioned him to addrefs me in the following manner.

"*Brother,*

"I have fomewhat to fay to you, and I hope you will not be offended when I tell you of your faults. You know that when you were reading your books in

13

town, I would not let the boys or any one difturb you; but now when I was praying, I faw you laughing. I do not think that you look upon praying as a foolifh thing;—I believe you pray yourfelf. But perhaps you may think my mode, or manner of prayer foolifh; if fo, you ought in a friendly manner to inftruct me, and not make fport of facred things."

I acknowledged my error, and on this he handed me his pipe to fmoke, in token of friendfhip and recon-ciliation; though at that time he had nothing to fmoke, but red-willow bark. I told him fomething of the method of reconciliation with an offended God, as re-vealed in my Bible, which I had then in poffeffion. He faid that he liked my ftory better than that of the French priefts, but he thought that he was now too old to begin to learn a new religion, therefore he fhould continue to worfhip God in the way that he had been taught, and that if falvation or future happinefs was to be had in his way of worfhip, he expected he would obtain it, and if it was inconfiftent with the honor of the great fpirit to accept of him in his own way of wor-fhip, he hoped that Owaneeyo would accept of him in the way I had mentioned, or in fome other way, though he might now be ignorant of the channel through which favor or mercy might be conveyed. He faid that he believed that Owaneeyo would hear and help every one that fincerely waited upon him.

Here we may fee how far the light of nature could

go; perhaps we fee it here almoft in its higheft extent. Notwithftanding the juft views that this great man entertained of Providence, yet we now fee him (though he acknowledged his guilt) expecting to appeafe the Deity, and procure his favor, by burning a little tobacco. We may obferve that all Heathen nations, as far as we can find out either by tradition or the light of Nature, agree with Revelation in this, that facrifice is neceffary, or that fome kind of atonement is to be made, in order to remove guilt, and reconcile them to God. This, accompanied with numberlefs other witneffes, is fufficient evidence of the rationality the truth of the Scriptures.

A few days after Tecaughretanego had gone through his ceremonies, and finifhed his prayers, the rain came and raifed the creek a fufficient height, fo that we paffed in fafety down to Sciota, and proceeded up to the carrying place. Let us now defcribe the land on this route, from our winter hut, and down Ollentangy to the Sciota, and up it to the carrying place.

About our winter cabbin is chiefly firft and fecond rate land. A confiderable way up Ollentangy on the fouthweft fide thereof, or betwixt it and the Miami, there is a very large prairie, and from this prairie down Ollentangy to Sciota, is generally firft rate land. The timber is walnut, fugar-tree, afh, buckeye, locuft, wild-cherry, and fpice-wood, intermixed with fome oak and beech. From the mouth of Ollentangy on the eaft fide of Sciota, up to the carrying place, there is a large body of firft and fecond rate land, and tolerably well watered. The timber is afh, fugar-tree, walnut, locuft, oak, and beech. Up near the carrying place, the land is a little hilly, but the foil good.

We proceeded from this place down Sandufky, and in our paffage we killed four bears, and a number of turkeys. Tecaughretanego appeared now fully per-fuaded that all this came in anfwer to his prayers—and who can fay with any degree of certainty that it was not fo?

When we came to the little lake at the mouth of San-dufky we called at a Wiandot town that was then there, called Sunyendeand. Here we diverted ourfelves fev-eral days, by catching rock-fifh in a fmall creek, the name of which is alfo Sunyendeand, which fignifies Rock-Fifh. They fifhed in the night, with lights, and ftruck the fifh with giggs or fpears. The rock-fifh here, when they begin firft to run up the creek to fpawn, are exceeding fat, and fufficient to fry themfelves. The firft night we fcarcely caught fifh enough for prefent ufe, for all that was in the town.

The next morning I met with a prifoner at this place, by the name of Thompfon, who had been taken from Virginia: he told me if the Indians would only omit difturbing the fifh for one night, he could catch more fifh than the whole town could make ufe of. I told Mr. Thompfon that if he was certain that he could do this, that I would ufe my influence with the Indians, to let the fifh alone for one night. I applied to the chiefs, who agreed to my propofal, and faid they were anxious to fee what the Great Knife (as they called the Virginian) could do. Mr. Thompfon, with the affiftance of fome other prifoners, fet to work, and made a hoop net of Elm bark: they then cut down a tree acrofs the creek, and ftuck in ftakes at the lower fide of it, to prevent the fifh from paffing up, leaving only a gap at the one fide of the creek:—here he fat with his net, and when he felt the fifh touch the net he drew it up, and frequently would hawl out two or three rock-fifh that would weigh about five or fix pounds each. He continued at this until he had hawled out about a waggon load, and then left the gap open, in order to let them pafs up, for they could not go far, on account of the fhallow water. Before day Mr. Thompfon fhut it up, to prevent them from paffing down, in order to let the Indians have fome diverfion in killing them in daylight.

When the news of the fifh came to town, the Indians all collected, and with furprize beheld the large heap of fifh, and applauded the ingenuity of the Virginian. When they faw the number of them that were confined in the water above the tree, the young Indians ran back to the town, and in a fhort time returned with their fpears, giggs, bows and arrows, &c. and were the chief of that day engaged in killing rock-fifh, infomuch that we had more than we could ufe or preferve. As we had

no falt, or any way to keep them, they lay upon the
banks, and after fome time great numbers of turkey-
buzzards and eagles collected together and devoured
them.

Shortly after this we left Sunyendeand, and in three
days arrived at Detroit, where we remained this fummer.

Some time in May we heard that General Forbes,
with feven thoufand men was preparing to carry on a
campaign againft Fort DuQuefne, which then ftood near
where Fort Pitt was afterwards erected.   Upon receiving this news a number of runners were fent off by the
French commander at Detroit, to urge the different
tribes of Indian warriors to repair to Fort DuQuefne.

Some time in July 1758, the Ottowas, Jibewas, Poto-
watomies and Wiandots rendezvoufed at Detroit, and
marched off to Fort DuQuefne, to prepare for the en-
counter of General Forbes.   The common report was,
that they would ferve him as they did General Braddock, and obtain much plunder.   From this time, until
fall, we had frequent accounts of Forbes's army, by
Indian runners that were fent out to watch their motion.
They fpied them frequently from the mountains ever
after they left Fort Loudon.   Notwithftanding their
vigilence, colonel Grant with his Highlanders ftole a
march upon them, and in the night took poffeffion of a
hill about eighty rod from Fort DuQuefne:—this hill
is on that account called Grant's hill to this day.   The

French and Indians knew not that Grant and his men were there until they beat the drum and played upon the bag-pipes, juſt at day-light. They then flew to arms, and the Indians ran up under covert of the banks of Allegheny and Monongahela, for ſome diſtance, and then ſallied out from the banks of the rivers, and took poſſeſſion of the hill above Grant; and as he was on the point of it in ſight of the fort, they immediately ſurrounded him, and as he had his Highlanders in ranks, and very cloſe order, and the Indians ſcattered, and concealed behind trees, they defeated him with the loſs only of a few warriors:—moſt of the Highlanders were killed or taken priſoners.

After this defeat the Indians held a council, but were divided in their opinions. Some ſaid that general Forbes would now turn back, and go home the way that he came, as Dunbar had done when General Braddock was defeated: others ſuppoſed he would come on. The French urged the Indians to ſtay and ſee the event: —but as it was hard for the Indians to be abſent from their ſquaws and children, at this ſeaſon of the year, a great many of them returned home to their hunting. After this, the remainder of the Indians, ſome French regulars, and a number of Canadians, marched off in queſt of General Forbes. They met his army near Fort Ligoneer, and attacked them, but were fruſtrated in their deſign. They ſaid that Forbes's men were beginning to learn the art of war, and that there were a

great number of American riflemen along with the red-
coats, who fcattered out, took trees, and were good
marks-men; therefore they found they could not accomplifh their defign, and were obliged to retreat. When
they returned from the battle to Fort DuQuefne, the
Indians concluded that they would go to their hunting.
The French endeavored to perfuade them to ftay and
try another battle. The Indians faid if it was only the
red-coats they had to do with, they could foon fubdue
them, but they could not withftand *Afhalecoa*, or the
Great Knife, which was the name they gave the Virginians. They then returned home to their hunting, and
the French evacuated the fort, which General Forbes
came and took poffeffion of without further oppofition,
late in the year 1758, and at this time began to build
Fort Pitt.

When Tecaughretanego had heard the particulars of
Grant's defeat, he faid that he could not well account
for his contradictory and inconfiftent conduct. He faid
as the art of war confifts in ambufhing and furprizing
our enemies, and in preventing them from ambufhing
and furprizing us; Grant, in the firft place, acted like a
wife and experienced officer, in artfully approaching in
the night without being difcovered; but when he came
to the place, and the Indians were lying afleep outfide
of the fort, between him and the Allegheny river, in
place of flipping up quietly, and falling upon them
with their broad fwords, they beat the drums and played

upon the bag-pipes. He faid he could account for this inconfiftent conduct no other way than by fuppofing that he had made too free with fpirituous liquors during the night, and became intoxicated about day-light. But to return:

This year we hunted up Sandufky, and down Sciota, took nearly the fame route that we had done the laft hunting feafon. We had confiderable fuccefs, and returned to Detroit fome time in April 1759.

Shortly after this, Tecaughretanego, his fon Nungany and myfelf, went from Detroit, (in an elm bark canoe) to Caughnewaga, a very ancient Indian town, about nine miles above Montreal, where I remained until about the firft of July. I then heard of a French fhip at Montreal that had Englifh prifoners on board, in order to carry them over fea, and exchange them. I went privately off from the Indians, and got alfo on board; but as general Wolfe had ftopped the River St. Laurence, we were all fent to prifon at Montreal, where I remained four months. Some time in November we were all fent off from this place to Crown Point, and exchanged.

Early in the year 1760, I came home to Conococheague, and found that my people could never afcertain whether I was killed or taken, until my return. They received me with great joy, but were furprifed to fee me fo much like an Indian, both in my gait and gefture.

14

Upon enquiry; I found that my fweet-heart was married a few days before I arrived. My feelings I muft leave on this occafion, for thofe of my readers to judge, who have felt the pangs of difappointed love, as it is impoffible now for me to defcribe the emotion of foul I felt at that time.

Now there was peace with the Indians which lafted until the year 1763. Sometime in May, this year, I married, and about that time the Indians again commenced hoftilities, and were bufily engaged in killing and fcalping the frontier inhabitants in various parts of Pennfylvania. The whole Conococheague Valley, from the North to the South Mountain, had been almoft entirely evacuated during Braddock's war. This ftate was then a Quaker government, and at the firft of this war the frontiers received no affiftance from the ftate. As the people were now beginning to live at home again, they thought hard to be drove away a fecond time, and were determined if poffible, to make a ftand: therefore they raifed as much money by collections and fubfcriptions, as would pay a company of rifle-men for feveral months. The fubfcribers met and elected a committee to manage the bufinefs. The committee appointed me captain of this company of rangers, and gave me the appointment of my fubalterns. I chofe two of the moft active young men that I could find, who had alfo been long in captivity with the Indians. As we enlifted our men, we dreffed them uniformly in the Indian manner, with breech-clouts, leggins, mockefons and green fhrouds, which we wore in the fame manner that the Indians do, and nearly as the Highlanders wear their plaids. In place of hats we wore red handkerchiefs, and painted our faces red and black, like Indian warriors. I taught them the Indian difcipline, as I knew of no other at that time, which would anfwer the purpofe much better than Britifh. We fucceeded beyond expectation in defending the frontiers, and were extolled by our employers. Near the conclufion of this expedition, I accepted of an enfign's commiffion in the regular fervice, under King George, in what was then called the Pennfylvania line. Upon my refignation, my lieutenant fucceeded me in command, the reft of the time they were to ferve. In the fall (the fame year) I went on the Sufquehannah campaign, againft the Indians, under the command of General Armftrong. In this route we burnt the Delaware and Monfey towns, on the Weft Branch of the Sufquehannah, and deftroyed all their corn.

In the year 1764, I received a lieutenant's commiffion, and went out on General Bouquet's campaign againft the Indians on the Mufkingum. Here we brought them to terms, and promifed to be at peace with them, upon condition that they would give up all our people that they had then in captivity among them. They then delivered unto us three hundred of the prifoners, and faid that they could not collect them all at this time, as it was now late in the year, and they were far fcattered; but they promifed that they would bring them all into Fort Pitt early next fpring, and as fecurity that they would do this, they delivered to us fix of their chiefs, as hoftages.   Upon this we fettled a ceffation of arms for fix months, and promifed upon their fulfilling the aforefaid condition, to make with them a permanent peace.

A little below Fort Pitt the hoftages all made their efcape.   Shortly after this the Indians ftole horfes, and killed fome people on the frontiers.   The king's proclamation was then circulating and fet up in various public places, prohibiting any perfon from trading with the Indians, until further orders.

Notwithftanding all this, about the firft of March 1765, a number of waggons loaded with Indian goods, and warlike ftores, were fent from Philadelphia to Henry Pollen's, Conococheague, and from thence feventy pack-horfes were loaded with thefe goods, in order to carry them to Fort Pitt.   This alarmed the country, and Mr. William Duffield raifed about fifty armed men, and met the pack-horfes at the place where Mercerfburg now ftands.   Mr. Duffield defired the employers to ftore up their goods, and not proceed until further orders.   They made light of this, and went over the North Mountain, where they lodged in a fmall valley called the Great Cove.   Mr. Duffield and his party followed after, and came to their lodging, and again urged them to ftore up their goods:—He reafoned with them on the impropriety of their proceedings, and the great danger the frontier inhabitants would be expofed to, if the Indians fhould now get a fupply:—He faid as it was well known that they had fcarcely any amunition, and were almoft naked, to fupply them now, would be a kind of murder, and would be illegally trading at the expence of the blood and treafure of the frontiers. Notwithftanding his powerful reafoning, thefe traders made game of what he faid, and would only anfwer him by ludicrous burlefque.

When I beheld this, and found that Mr. Duffield would not compel them to ftore up their goods, I collected ten of my old warriors, that I had formerly difciplined in the Indian way, went off privately, after night, and encamped in the woods. The next day, as ufual, we blacked and painted, and waylayed them near Sidelong Hill. I fcattered my men about forty rod along the fide of the road, and ordered every two to take a tree, and about eight or ten rod between each couple, with orders to keep a referve fire, one not to fire until his comrade had loaded his gun—by this means we kept up a conftant, flow fire, upon them from front to rear:—We then heard nothing of thefe trader's merriment or burlefque. When they faw their packhorfes falling clofe by them, they called out *pray gentlemen, what would you have us to do?* The reply was, *collect all your loads to the front, and unload them in one place; take your private property, and immediately retire.*

When they were gone, we burnt what they left, which confifted of blankets, fhirts, vermillion, lead, beads, wampum, tomahawks, fcalping knives, &c.

The·traders went back to Fort Loudon, and applied to the commanding officer there, and got a party of Highland foldiers, and went with them in queft of the robbers, as they called us, and without applying to a magiftrate, or obtaining any civil authority, but barely upon fufpicion, they took a number of creditable perfons prifoners, (who were chiefly not in any way concerned in this action) and confined them in the guard-houfe in Fort Loudon. I then raifed three hundred riflemen, marched to Fort Loudon, and encamped on a hill in fight of the fort. We were not long there, until we had more than double as many of the Britifh troops prifoners in our camp, as they had of our people in the guard-houfe. Captain Grant, a Highland officer, who commanded Fort Loudon, then fent a flag of truce to our camp, where we fettled a cartel, and gave them above two for one, which enabled us to redeem all our men from the guard-houfe, without further difficulty.

After this Captain Grant kept a number of rifle guns, which the Highlanders had taken from the country peo-ple, and refufed to give them up. As he was riding out one day, we took him prifoner, and detained him until he delivered up the arms; we alfo deftroyed a large quantity of gun-powder that the traders had ftored up, left it might be conveyed privately to the Indians. The

king's troops, and our party, had now got entirely out
of the channel of the civil law, and many unjuſtifiable
things were done by both parties.   This convinced me
more than ever I had been before, of the abſolute neces-
ſity of the civil law, in order to govern mankind.

About this time the following ſong was compoſed by
Mr. George Campbell (an Iriſh gentleman, who had
been educated in Dublin) and was frequently ſung to
the tune of the Black Joke:

> 1. Ye patriot ſouls who love to ſing,
>   What ſerves your country and your king,
>   In wealth, peace and royal eſtate ;
>   Attention give whilſt I rehearſe,
>   A modern faĉt, in jingling verſe,
>   How party intereſt ſtrove what it cou'd,
>   To profit itſelf by public blood,
>   But juſtly met its merited fate.

> 2. Let all thoſe Indian traders claim,
>   Their juſt reward, inglorious fame,
>   For vile baſe and treacherous ends.
>   To Pollins, in the ſpring they ſent,
>   Much warlike ſtores, with an intent,
>   To carry them to our barbarous foes,
>   Expeĉting that no-body dare oppoſe,
>   A preſent to their Indian friends.

> 3. Aſtoniſh'd at the wild deſign,
>   Frontier inhabitants combin'd,
>   With brave ſouls, to ſtop their career,

Although fome men apoftatiz'd,
Who firft the grand attempt advis'd,
The bold frontiers they bravely ftood,
To act for their king and their country's good,
　　In joint league, and ftrangers to fear.

4. On March the fifth, in fixty-five,
Their Indian prefents did arrive,
　　In long pomp and cavalcade,
Near Sidelong Hill, where in difguife,
Some patriots did their train furprize,
And quick as lightning tumbled their loads,
And kindled them bonfires in the woods,
　　And moftly burnt their whole brigade.

5. At Loudon, when they heard the news,
They fcarcely knew which way to choofe,
　　For blind rage and difcontent ;
At length fome foldiers they fent out,
With guides for to conduct the route,
And feized fome men that were trav'ling there,
And hurried them into Loudon where
　　They laid them faft with one confent.

6. But men of refolution thought,
Too much to fee their neighbors caught,
　　For no crime but falfe furmife ;
Forthwith they join'd a warlike band,
And march'd to Loudon out of hand,
And kept the jailors prif'ners there,
Until our friends enlarged were,
　　Without fraud or any difguife.

7. Let mankind cenfure or commend,
   This rafh performance in the end,
      Then both fides will find their account.
   'Tis true no law can juftify,
   To burn our neighbors property,
   But when this property is defign'd,
   To ferve the enemies of mankind,
      It's high treafon in the amount.

After this we kept up a guard of men on the fron-tiers, for feveral months, to prevent fupplies being fent to the Indians, until it was proclaimed that Sir William Johnfon had made peace with them, and then we let the traders pafs unmolefted.

In the year 1766, I heard that Sir William Johnfon, the king's agent for fettling affairs with the Indians, had purchafed from them all the land weft of the Appa-lachian Mountains, that lay between the Ohio and the Cherokee River; and as I knew by converfing with the Indians in their own tongue, that there was a large body of rich land there, I concluded I would take a tour weft-ward, and explore that country.

I fet out about the laft of June, 1766, and went in the firft place to Holftein River, and from thence I travelled weftward in company with Jofhua Horton, Uriah Stone, William Baker, and James Smith, who came from near Carlifle. There was only four white men of us, and a mulatto flave about eighteen years of

15

age, that Mr. Horton had with him. We explored the country fouth of Kentucky, and there was no more fign of white men there then, than there is now weft of the head waters of the Miffouri. We alfo explored Cumberland and Tenneffee Rivers, from Stone's* River down to the Ohio.

When we came to the mouth of Tenneffee my fellow travellers concluded that they would proceed on to the Illinois, and fee fome more of the land to the weft:—this I would not agree to. As I had already been longer from home than what I expected, I thought my wife would be diftreffed, and think I was killed by the Indians; therefore I concluded that I would return home. I fent my horfe with my fellow travellers to the Illinois, as it was difficult to take a horfe through the mountains. My comrades gave me the greateft part of the amunition they then had, which amounted only to half a pound of powder, and lead equivalent. Mr. Horton alfo lent me his mulatto boy, and I then fet off through the wildernefs, for Carolina.

About eight days after I left my company at the mouth of Tenneffee, on my journey eaftward, I got a cane ftab in my foot, which occafioned my leg to fwell, and I fuffered much pain. I was now in a doleful fitu-

---

* Stone's River is a fouth branch of Cumberland, and empties into it above Nafhville. We firft gave it this name in our journal in May 1767, after one of my fellow travellers, Mr. Uriah Stone, and I am told that it retains the fame name unto this day.

ation—far from any of the human fpecies, excepting black Jamie, or the favages, and I knew not when I might meet with them—my cafe appeared defperate, and I thought fomething muft be done. All the furgical inftruments I had, was a knife, a mockafon awl, and a pair of bullit moulds—with thefe I determined to draw the fnag from my foot, if poffible. I ftuck the awl in the fkin, and with the knife I cut the flefh away from around the cane, and then I commanded the mulatto fellow to catch it with the bullit moulds, and pull it out, which he did. When I faw it, it feemed a fhocking thing to be in any perfon's foot; it will therefore be fuppofed that I was very glad to have it out. The black fellow attended upon me, and obeyed my directions faithfully. I ordered him to fearch for Indian medicine, and told him to get me a quantity of bark from the root of a lynn tree, which I made him beat on a ftone, with a tomahawk, and boil it in a kettle, and with the ooze I bathed my foot and leg:—what remained when I had finifhed bathing, I boiled to a jelly, and made poultices thereof. As I had no rags, I made ufe of the green mofs that grows upon logs, and wrapped it round with elm bark: by this means (fimple as it may feem) the fwelling and inflamation in a great meafure abated. As ftormy weather appeared, I ordered Jamie to make us a fhelter, which he did by erecting forks and poles, and covering them over with cane tops, like a fodder-houfe. It was but about one hundred yards from a large buffaloe road. As we were almoſt out of proviſion, I commanded Jamie to take my gun, and I went along as well as I could, concealed myſelf near the road, and killed a buffaloe. When this was done, we jirked* the lean, and fryed the tallow out of the fat meat, which we kept to ſtew with our jirk as we needed it.

While I lay at this place, all the books I had to read, was a Pſalm Book, and Watts upon Prayer. Whilſt in this ſituation I compoſed the following verſes, which I then frequently ſung.

1. Six weeks I've in this deſart been,
    With one mulatto lad,
  Excepting this poor ſtupid ſlave,
    No company I had.

2. In ſolitude I here remain,
    A cripple very ſore,
  No friend or neighbor to be found,
    My caſe for to deplore.

3. I'm far from home, far from the wife,
    Which in my boſom lay,
  Far from my children dear, which uſed
    Around me for to play.

---

* Jirk is a name well known by the hunters, and frontier inhabitants, for meat cut in ſmall pieces and laid on a ſcaffold, over a ſlow fire, whereby it is roaſted till it is thoroughly dry.

4. This doleful circumſtance cannot
    My happineſs prevent,
While peace of conſcience I enjoy,
    Great comfort and content.

I continued in this place until I could walk ſlowly, without crutches. As I now lay near a great buffaloe road, I was afraid that the Indians might be paſſing that way, and diſcover my fire-place, therefore I moved off ſome diſtance, where I remained until I killed an elk. As my foot was yet ſore, I concluded that I would ſtay here until it was healed, leſt by travelling too ſoon it might again be inflamed.

In a few weeks after, I proceeded on, and in October I arrived in Carolina. I had now been eleven months in the wilderneſs, and during this time I neither ſaw bread, money, women, or ſpirituous liquors; and three months of which I ſaw none of the human ſpecies, except Jamie.

When I came into the ſettlement my clothes were almoſt worn out, and the boy had nothing on him that ever was ſpun. He had buck-ſkin leggins, mockaſons, and breech-clout—a bear-ſkin dreſſed with the hair on, which he belted about him, and a racoon-ſkin cap. I had not travelled far after I came in before I was ſtrictly examined by the inhabitants. I told them the truth, and where I came from, &c. but my ſtory appeared ſo ſtrange to them, that they did not believe me. They faid they had never heard of any one coming through the mountains from the mouth of Tenneffee; and if any one would undertake fuch a journey, furely no man would lend him his flave. They faid that they thought that all I had told them were lies, and on fufpicion they took me into cuftody, and fet a guard over me.

While I was confined here, I met with a reputable old acquaintance, who voluntarily became my voucher; and alfo told me of a number of my acquaintances that now lived near this place, who had moved from Pennfylvania—On this being made public, I was liberated. I went to a magiftrate, and obtained a pafs, and one of my old acquaintances made me a prefent of a fhirt. I then caft away my old rags, and all the clothes I now had was an old beaver hat, buck-fkin leggins, mockafons, and a new fhirt; alfo an old blanket, which I commonly carried on my back in good weather. Being thus equipped, I marched on, with my white fhirt loofe, and Jamie with his bear-fkin about him:—myfelf appearing white, and Jamie very black, alarmed the dogs where-ever we came, fo that they barked violently. The people frequently came out and afked me where we came from, &c. I told them the truth, but they, for the moft part fufpected my ftory, and I generally had to fhew them my pafs. In this way I came on to Fort Chiffel, where I left Jamie at Mr. Horton's negro-quarter, according to promife. I went from thence to Mr. George Adams's, on Reed Creek, where I had lodged, and where I had left my clothes, as I was going out from home. When I dreffed myfelf in good clothes, and mounted on horfeback, no man ever afked me for a pafs; therefore I concluded that a horfe-thief, or even a robber, might pafs without interruption, provided he was only well-dreffed, whereas the fhabby villain would be immediately detected.

I returned home to Conococheague, in the fall 1767. When I arrived, I found that my wife and friends had defpaired of ever feeing me again, as they had heard that I was killed by the Indians, and my horfe brought into one of the Cherokee towns.

In the year 1769, the Indians again made incurfions on the frontiers; yet, the traders continued carrying goods and warlike ftores to them. The frontiers took the alarm, and a number of perfons collected, deftroyed and plundered a quantity of their powder, lead, &c. in Bedford county. Shortly after this, fome of thefe perfons, with others, were apprehended and laid in irons in the guard-houfe in Fort Bedford, on fufpicion of being the perpetrators of this crime.

Though I did not altogether approve of the conduct of this new club of black-boys, yet I concluded that they fhould not lie in irons in the guard-houfe, or remain in confinement, by arbitrary or military power. I refolved therefore, if poffible, to releafe them, if they even fhould be tried by the civil law afterwards. I collected eighteen of my old black-boys, that I had feen tried in the Indian war, &c. I did not defire a large party, left they fhould be too much alarmed at Bedford, and accordingly prepare for us. We marched along the public road in day-light, and made no fecret of our defign:—We told thofe whom we met, that we were going to take Fort Bedford, which appeared to them a very unlikely ftory. Before this I made it known to one William Thompfon, a man whom I could truft, and who lived there: him I employed as a fpy, and fent him along on horfe-back, before, with orders to meet me at a certain place near Bedford, one hour before day. The next day a little before fun-fet we encamped near the croffings of Juniata, about fourteen miles from Bedford, and erected tents, as though we intended ftaying all night, and not a man in my company knew to the contrary, fave myfelf. Knowing that they would hear this in Bedford, and wifhing it to be the cafe, I thought to furprize them, by ftealing a march.

As the moon rofe about eleven o'clock, I ordered my boys to march, and we went on at the rate of five miles an hour, until we met Thompfon at the place appointed. He told us that the commanding officer had frequently heard of us by travellers, and had ordered thirty men upon guard. He faid they knew our number, and only made game of the notion of eighteen men coming to refcue the prifoners, but they did not expect us until towards the middle of the day. I afked him if the gate was open? He faid it was then fhut, but he expected they would open it as ufual, at day-light, as they apprehended no danger. I then moved my men privately up under the banks of Juniata, where we lay concealed about one hundred yards from the fort gate. I had ordered the men to keep a profound filence, until we got into it. I then fent off Thompfon again to fpy. At day-light he returned, and told us that the gate was open, and three centinels were ftanding on the wall— that the guards were taking a morning dram, and the arms ftanding together in one place. I then concluded to rufh into the fort, and told Thompfon to run before me to the arms, we ran with all our might, and as it was a mifty morning, the centinels fcarcely faw us until we were within the gate, and took poffeffion of the arms. Juft as we were entering, two of them difcharged their guns, though I do not believe they aimed at us. We then raifed a fhout, which furprized the town, though fome of them were well pleafed with the news. We compelled a black-fmith to take the irons off the prif- oners, and then we left the place. This, I believe, was the firft Britifh fort in America, that was taken by what they called American rebels.

Some time after this I took a journey weftward, in order to furvey fome located land I had on and near the You- hogany. As I paffed near Bedford, while I was walk- ing and leading my horfe, I was overtaken by fome men on horfe-back, like travellers. One of them afked my name, and on telling it, they immediately pulled out

16

their piftols, and prefented them at me, calling upon me
to deliver myfelf, or I was a dead man.   I ftepped back,
prefented my rifle, and told them to ftand off.   One of
them fnapped a piftol at me, and another was preparing
to fhoot, when I fired my piece:—one of them alfo
fired near the fame time, and one of my fellow travellers fell.   The affailants then rufhed up, and as my gun
was empty, they took and tied me.   I charged them
with killing my fellow traveller, and told them he was
a man that I had accidentally met with on the road, that
had nothing to do with the public quarrel.   They af-
ferted that I had killed him.   I told them that my gun
blowed, or made a flow fire—that I had her from my
face before fhe went off, or I would not have miffed
my mark; and from the pofition my piece was in when
it went off, it was not likely that my gun killed this
man, yet I acknowledged I was not certain that it was
not fo.   They then carried me to Bedford, laid me in
irons in the guard-houfe, fummoned a jury of the
oppofite party, and held an inqueft.   The jury brought
me in guilty of wilful murder.   As they were afraid to
keep me long in Bedford, for fear of a refcue, they fent
me privately through the wildernefs to Carlifle, where
I was laid in heavy irons.

Shortly after I came here, we heard that a number of
my old black-boys were coming to tear down the jail.
I told the fheriff that I would not be refcued, as I knew
that the indictment was wrong; therefore I wifhed to ftand

my trial. As I had found the black boys to be always under good command, I expected I could prevail on them to return, and therefore wifhed to write to them— to this the fheriff readily agreed. I wrote a letter to them, with irons on my hands, which was immediately fent; but as they had heard that I was in irons, they would come on. When we heard they were near the town, I told the fheriff I would fpeak to them out of the window, and if the irons were off, I made no doubt but I could prevail on them to defift. The fheriff ordered them to be taken off, and juft as they were taken off my hands, the black boys came running up to the jail. I went to the window and called to them, and they gave attention. I told them as my indictment was for wilful murder, to admit of being refcued, would appear difhonorable. I thanked them for their kind intentions, and told them the greateft favor they could confer upon me, would be to grant me this one requeft, *to withdraw from the jail, and return in peace*; to this they complied, and withdrew. While I was fpeaking, the irons were taken off my feet, and never again put on.

Before this party arrived at Conococheague, they met about three hundred more, on the way, coming to their affiftance, and were refolved to take me out; they then turned, and all came together, to Carlifle. The reafon they gave for coming again, was, becaufe they thought that government was fo enraged at me that I would not get a fair trial; but my friends and myfelf together again prevailed on them to return in peace.

At this time the public papers were partly filled with thefe occurrences. The following is an extract from the Pennfylvania Gazette, number 2132, November 2d, 1769.

"*Conococheague, October* 16th, 1769.

"Mess. Hall & Sellers,

"Pleafe to give the following narrative a place in your Gazette, and you will much oblige

"Your humble fervant,

"WILLIAM SMITH."

"Whereas, in this Gazette of September 28th, 1769, there appeared an extract of a letter from Bedford, September 12th, 1769, relative to James Smith, as being apprehended on fufpicion of being a black boy, then killing his companion, &c. I look upon myfelf as bound by all the obligations of truth, juftice to character and to the world, to fet that matter in a true light; by which, I hope the impartial world will be enabled to obtain a more juft opinion of the prefent fcheme of acting in this end of the country, as alfo to form a true idea of the truth, candor, and ingenuity of the author of the faid extract, in ftating that matter in fo partial a light. The ftate of the cafe (which can be made appear by undeniable evidence,) was this: "James Smith, (who is ftiled the principal ring leader of the black boys, by the said author) together with his younger brother, and brother-in-law, were going out in order to furvey and improve their land on the waters of Youghoghany, and as the time of their return was long, they took with them their arms, and horfes loaded with the neceffaries of life: and as one of Smith's brothers-in-law was an artift in furveying, he had alfo with him the inftruments for that bufinefs. Travelling on the way, within about nine miles of Bedford, they overtook, and joined company with one Johnfon and Moorhead, who likewife had horfes loaded, part of which loading was liquor, and part feed wheat, their intentions being to make improvements on their lands. When they arrived at the parting of the road on this fide of Bedford, the company feparated, one part going through the town, in order to get a horfe fhod, were apprehended, and put under confinement, but for what crime they knew not, and treated in a manner utterly inconfiftent with the laws of their country, and the liberties of Englifhmen :—Whilft the other part, viz. James Smith, Johnfon and Moorhead, taking along the other road, were met by John Holmes efq. to whom James Smith fpoke in a friendly manner, but received no anfwer. Mr. Holmes hafted, and gave an alarm in Bedford, from whence a party of men were fent in purfuit of them; but Smith and his companions not having the leaft thought of any fuch meafures being taken, (why fhould they?) travelled flowly on. After they had gained the place where the roads joined, they

delayed until the other part of their company fhould
come up.   At this time a number of men came riding,
like men travelling ; they afked Smith his name, which
he told them—on which they immediately affaulted him
as highway-men, and with prefented piftols, commanded
him to furrender, or he was a dead man ; upon which
Smith ftepped back, afked them if they were highway-
men, charging them at the fame time to ftand off, when
immediately, Robert George (one of the affailants)
fnapped a piftol at Smith's head, and that before Smith
offered to fhoot, (which faid George himfelf acknowledged upon oath;) whereupon Smith prefented his gun
at another of the affailants, who was preparing to fhoot
him with his piftol.   The faid affailant having a hold
of Johnfon by the arm, two fhots were fired, one by
Smith's gun, the other from a piftol fo quick as juft to
be diftinguifhable, and Johnfon fell.   After which Smith
was taken and carried into Bedford, where John Holmes,
efq. the informer, held an inqueft on the corpfe, one of
the affailants being as an evidence, (nor was there any
other trouble about the matter) Smith was brought in
guilty of wilful murder, and fo committed to prifon.
But a jealoufy arifing in the breafts of many that the
inqueft, either through inadvertency, ignorance or fome
other default, was not fo fair as it ought to be ; William Deny, coroner of the county, upon requifition
made, thought proper to re-examine the matter, and
fummoning a jury of unexceptionable men, out of three

townſhips—men whoſe candor, probity and honeſty, is unqueſtionable with all who are acquainted with them, and having raiſed the corpſe, held an inqueſt in a ſolemn manner, during three days. In the courſe of their ſcrutiny they found Johnſon's ſhirt blacked about the bullit-hole, by the powder of the charge by which he was killed, whereupon they examined into the diſtance Smith ſtood from Johnſon when he ſhot, and one of the aſſailants being admitted to oath, ſwore to the reſpeĉtive ſpots of ground they both ſtood on at that time, which the jury meaſured, and found to be twenty-three feet, nearly ; then trying the experiment of ſhooting at the ſame ſhirt, both with and againſt the wind, and at the ſame diſtance, found no effeĉts, not the leaſt ſtain from the powder, on the ſhirt:—And let any perſon that pleaſes, make the experiment, and I will venture to affirm he ſhall find that powder will not ſtain at half the diſtance above mentioned, ʳif ſhot out of a rifle gun, which Smith's was. Upon the whole, the jury, after the moſt accurate examination, and mature deliberation, brought in their verdiĉt that ſome one of the aſſailants themſelves muſt neceſſarily have been the perpetrators of the murder.

" I have now repreſented the matter in its true and genuine colors, and which I will abide by. I only beg liberty to make a few remarks and refleĉtions on the above mentioned extraĉt. The author ſays " James Smith, with two others in company, paſſed round the town,

without touching," by which it is plain he would infin-
uate, and make the public believe that Smith, and that
part of the company, had taken fome bye road, which
is utterly falfe, for it was the king's high-way, and the
ftraighteft, that through Bedford, being fomething to
the one fide, nor would the other part of the company
have gone through the town, but for the reafon already
given. Again, the author fays that "four men were
fent in purfuit of Smith and his companions, who overtook them about five miles from Bedford, and commanded them to furrender, on which Smith prefented
his gun at one of the men, who was ftruggling with his
companion, fired it at him, and fhot his companion
through the back." Here I would juft remark again,
the unfair and partial account given of this matter, by
the author; not a word mentioned of George's fnapping
his piftol before Smith offered to fhoot, or of another
of the affailants actually firing his piftol, though he con-
feffed himfelf afterwards, he had done fo; not the leaft
mention of the company's baggage, which, to men in
the leaft open to a fair inquiry, would have been fufficient proof of the innocence of their intentions. Muft
not an effufive blufh overfpread the face of the partial
reprefenter of facts, when he finds the veil he had thrown
over truth thus pulled afide, and fhe expofed to naked
view. Suppofe it fhould be granted that Smith fhot
the man, (which is not, and I prefume never can be
proven to be the cafe) I would only afk, was he not on

his own defence ? Was he not publicly affaulted ? Was he not charged at the peril of his life, to furrender, without knowing for what ? No warrant being fhown him, or any declaration made of their authority. And feeing thefe things are fo, would any judicious man, any perfon in the leaft acquainted with the laws of the land, or morality, judge him guilty of wilful murder ? But I humbly prefume every one who has an opportunity of feeing this, will by this time be convinced that the proceedings againft Smith were truly unlawful and tyranical, perhaps unparalleled by any inftance in a civilized nation; for to endeavor to kill a man in the apprehending him, in order to bring him to trial for a fact, and that too on a fuppofed one, is undoubtedly beyond all bounds of law or government.

"If the author of the extract thinks I have treated him unfair, or that I have advanced any thing he can controvert, let him come forward as a fair antagonift, and make his defence, and I will, if called upon, vindicate all that I have advanced againft him or his abettors.

"WILLIAM SMITH."

I remained in prifon four months, and during this time I often thought of thofe that were confined in the time of the perfecution, who declared their prifon was converted into a palace. I now learned what this meant, as I never fince, or before, experienced four months of equal happinefs.

17

When the fupreme court fat, I was feverely profecu-
ted. At the commencement of my trial, the judges in
a very unjuft and arbitrary manner, rejected feveral of
my⁷ evidences ; yet, as Robert George (one of thofe
who were in the fray when I was taken) fwore in court
that he fnapped a piftol at me before I fhot, and a con-
currence of corroborating circumftances, amounted to
ftrong prefumptive evident that it could not poffibly be
my gun that killed Johnfon, the jury, without hefita-
tion, brought in their verdict, NOT GUILTY. One
of the judges then declared that not one of this jury
fhould ever hold any office above a conftable. Notwithftanding this proud, ill-natured declaration, fome
of thefe jurymen afterwards filled honorable places, and
I myfelf was elected the next year, and fat on the board*
in Bedford county, and afterwards I ferved in the board
three years in Weftmoreland county.

In the year 1774, another Indian war commenced,
though at this time the white people were the aggreffors.
The profpect of this terrified the frontier inhabitants,
infomuch that the greater part on the Ohio waters,
either fled over the mountains, eaftward, or collected
into forts. As the ftate of Pennfylvania apprehended
great danger, they at this time appointed me captain
over what was then called the Pennfylvania line. As

---

* A board of commiffioners was annually elected in Pennfylvania, to
regulate taxes, and lay the county levy.

they knew I could raife men that would anfwer their purpofe, they feemed to lay afide their former inveteracy.

In the year 1776, I was appointed a major in the Pennfylvania affociation. When American independence was declared, I was elected a member of the convention in Weftmoreland county, ftate of Pennfylvania, and of the affembly as long as I propofed to ferve.

While I attended the affembly in Philadelphia, in the year 1777, I faw in the ftreet, fome of my old boys, on their way to the Jerfeys, againft the Britifh, and they defired me to go with them—I petitioned the houfe for leave of abfence, in order to head a fcouting party, which was granted me. We marched into the Jerfeys, and went before General Wafhington's army, way-laid the road at Rocky Hill, attacked about two hundred of the Britifh, and with thirty-fix men drove them out of the woods into a large open field. After this we attacked a party that were guarding the officers baggage, and took the waggon and twenty-two Heffians; and alfo re-took fome of our continental foldiers which they had with them. In a few days we killed and took more of the Britifh, than was of our party. At this time I took the camp fever, and was carried in a ftage waggon to Burlington, where I lay until I recovered. When I took fick, my companion, Major James M'Common, took the command of the party, and had greater ʻfuccefs than I had. If every officer and his party that lifted arms againſt the Englifh, had fought with the fame fuccefs that Major M'Common did, we would have made ſhort work of the Britiſh war.

When I returned to Philadelphia, I applied to the affembly for leave to raife a battallion of riflemen, which they appeared very willing to grant, but faid they could not do it, as the power of raifing men and commiſſioning officers was at that time committed to General Waſhington, therefore they advifed me to apply to his excellency. The following is a true copy of a letter of recommendation which I received at this time, from the council of fafety :

"IN COUNCIL OF SAFETY,

"Philadelphia, February 10*th,* 1777.

"SIR,

"Application has been made to us by James Smith efq. of Weſtmoreland, a gentleman well acquainted with the Indian cuſtoms, and their manners of carrying on war, for leave to raife a battallion of marks-men, expert in the ufe of rifles, and fuch as are acquainted with the Indian method of fighting, to be dreffed entirely in their faſhion, for the purpofe of annoying and harraſſing the enemy in their marches and encampments. We think two or three hundred men in that way, might be very ufeful. Should your excellency be of the fame opinion, and direct fuch a corps to be formed, we will take proper meafures for raifing the men on the frontiers of this ftate, and follow fuch other directions as your excellency fhall give in this matter.

" *To his excellency General Wafhington.*"

" The foregoing is a copy of a letter to his excellency General Wafhington, from the council of fafety.

"JACOB S. HOWELL,

"*Secretary.*"

After this I received another letter of recommenda- tion, which is as follows:

"We, whofe names are under written, do certify that James Smith (now of the county of Weftmoreland) was taken prifoner by the Indians, in an expedition before General Braddock's defeat, in the year 1755, and remained with them until the year 1760: and alfo that he ferved as enfign, in the year 1763, under the pay of the province of Pennfylvania, and as lieutenant, in the year 1764, and as captain, in the year 1774; and as a military officer he has fuftained a good character. And we do recommend him as a perfon well acquainted with the Indian's method of fighting, and, in our humble opinion, exceedingly fit for the command of a ranging or fcouting party, which we are alfo humbly of opinion, he could (if legally authorized) foon raife.   Given under our hands at Philadelphia, this 13th day of March, 1777.

Thomas Paxton, capt.	*John Procter, col.*
William Duffield, esq.	*Jonathan Hoge, esq.*
David Robb, esq.	*William Parker, capt.*
John Piper, col.	*Robert Elliot,*
William M'Comb.	*Joseph Armstrong, col.*
William Pepper, lieut. col.	*Robert Peebles, lieut. col.*
James M'Clane, esq.	*Samuel Patton, capt.*
	William Lyon, esq."

With thefe, and fome other letters of recommendation, which I have not now in my poffeffion, I went to his excellency, who lay at Morriftown.   Though General Wafhington did not fall in with the fcheme of white men turning Indians, yet he propofed giving me a major's place in a battallion of riflemen already raifed. I thanked the general for his propofal; but as I entertained no high opinion of the colonel that I was to ferve under, and with him I had no profpect of getting my old boys again, I thought I would be of more ufe in the caufe we were then ftruggling to fupport, to remain with them as a militia officer, therefore I did not accept this offer.

In the year 1778, I received a colonel's commiffion, and after my return to Weftmoreland, the Indians made an attack upon our frontiers.   I then raifed men and

purfued them, and the fecond day we overtook and defeated them. We likewife took four fcalps, and recovered the horfes and plunder which they were carrying
off. At the time of this attack, Captain John Hink-
fton purfued an Indian, both their guns being empty,
and after the fray was over he was miffing:—While we
were enquiring about him, he came walking up, feem-
ingly unconcerned, with a bloody fcalp in his hand—he
had purfued the Indian about a quarter of a mile, and
tomahawked him.

Not long after this I was called upon to command
four hundred riflemen, on an expedition againft the
Indian town on French Creek. It was fome time in
November before I received orders from General M'Intofh, to march, and then we were poorly equipped, and
fcarce of provifions. We marched in three columns,
forty rod from each other. There were alfo flankers
on the outfide of each column, that marched a-breaft in
the rear, in fcattered order—and even in the columns,
the men were one rod apart—and in the front, the volunteers marched a-breaft, in the fame manner of the
flankers, fcouring the woods. In cafe of an attack, the
officers were immediately to order the men to face out
and take trees—in this pofition the Indians could not
avail themfelves by furrounding us, or have an opportunity of fhooting a man from either fide of the tree.
If attacked, the center column was to reinforce whatever part appeared to require it the moft. When we

encamped, our encampment formed a hollow fquare, including about thirty or forty acres—on the outfide of the fquare there were centinels placed, whofe bufinefs it was to watch for the enemy, and fee that neither horfes or bullocks went out:—And when encamped, if any attacks were made by an enemy, each officer was immediately to order the men to face out and take trees, as before mentioned; and in this form they could not take the advantage by furrounding us, as they commonly had done when they fought the whites.

The following is a copy of general orders, given at this time, which I have found among my journals:

"AT CAMP—OPPOSITE FORT PITT,

"*November* 29*th*, 1778.

"GENERAL ORDERS:

"*A copy thereof is to be given to each captain and subaltern, and to be read to each company.*

"You are to march in three columns, with flankers on the front and rear, and to keep a profound filence, and not to fire a gun, except at the enemy, without particular orders for that purpofe; and in cafe of an attack, let it be fo ordered that every other man only, is to fhoot at once, excepting on extraordinary occafions. The one half of the men to keep a referve fire, until their comrades load; and let every one be particularly careful not to fire at any time without a view of the enemy, and that not at too great a diftance. I earneftly urge the above caution, as I have known very remarkable and grevious errors of this kind. You are to encamp on the hollow fquare, except the volunteers, who, according to their own requeft, are to encamp on the front of the fquare, a fufficient number of centinels are to be kept round the fquare at a proper diftance. Every man is to be under arms at the break of day, and to parade oppofite to their fire places, facing out, and when the officers examine their arms and find them in good order, and give neceffary directions, they are to be difmiffed, with orders to have their arms near them, and be always in readinefs.

"Given by
"JAMES SMITH, *Colonel.*"

In this manner we proceeded on, to French Creek, where we found the Indian town evacuated. I then went on further than my orders called for, in queft of Indians; but our provifions being nearly exhaufted, we were obliged to return. On our way back we met with confiderable difficulties on account of high waters and fcarcity of provifion; yet we never loft one horfe, excepting fome that gave out.

After peace was made with the Indians, I met with fome of them in Pittfburg, and enquired of them in their own tongue, concerning this expedition,—not letting them know I was there. They told me that they watched the movements of this army ever after they had left Fort-Pitt, and as they paffed thro the glades or barrens they had a full view of them from the adjacent hills, and computed their number to be about one thoufand. They faid they alfo examined their camps, both before and after they were gone, and found, they could not make an advantageous attack, and therefore moved off from their town and hunting ground before we arrived.

In the year 1788 I fettled in Bourbon county, Kentucky, feven miles above Paris; and in the fame year was elected a member of the convention that fat at Danville, to confer about a feparation from the ftate of Virginia;—and from that year until the year 1799, I reprefented Bourbon county, either in convention or as a member of the general affembly, except two years that I was left a few votes behind.

ON THE MANNERS AND CUSTOMS OF THE INDIANS.

The Indians are a flovenly people in their drefs.—They feldom ever wafh their fhirts, and in regard to cookery they are exceeding filthy. When they kill a buffaloe they will fometimes lafh the paunch of it round a fapling, and caft it into the kettle, boil it and fup the broth; tho they commonly fhake it about in cold water, then boil and eat it.—Notwithftanding all this, they are very polite in their own way, and they retain among them, the effentials of good manners; tho they have few compliments, yet they are complaifant to one another, and when accompanied with good humor and difcretion, they entertain ftrangers in the beft manner their circum-ftances will admit. They ufe but few titles of honor. In the military line, the titles of great men are only captains or leaders of parties—In the civil line, the titles are only councilors, chiefs or the old wifemen. Thefe titles are never made ufe of in addreffing any of their great men. The language commonly made ufe of in addreffing them, is, Grandfather, Father, or Uncle. They have no fuch thing in ufe among them, as Sir, Mr. Madam or Miftrefs—The common mode of

addreſs, is, my Friend, Brother, Couſin, or Mother, Sister, &c. They pay great reſpect to age; or to the aged
Fathers and Mothers among them of every rank. No
one can arrive at any place of honor, among them, but
by merit. Either ſome exploit in war, muſt be performed, before any one can be advanced in the military
line, or become eminent for wiſdom before they can
obtain a ſeat in council. It would appear to the
Indians a moſt ridiculous thing to ſee a man lead off a
company of warriors, as an officer, who had himſelf
never been in a battle in his life: even in caſe of merit,
they are ſlow in advancing any one, until they arrive at
or near middle-age.

They invite every one that comes to their houſe, or
camp to eat, while they have any thing to give; and it
is accounted bad manners to refuſe eating, when invited.
They are very tenacious of their old mode of dreſſing
and painting, and do not change their faſhions as we do.
They are very fond of tobacco, and the men almoſt all
ſmoke it mixed with ſumach leaves or red willow bark,
pulverized; tho they ſeldom uſe it any other way.
They make uſe of the pipe alſo as a token of love and
friendſhip.

In courtſhip they alſo differ from us. It is a common thing among them for a young woman, if in love,
to make ſuit to a young man; tho the firſt addreſs may
be by the man; yet the other is the moſt common.
The ſquaws are generally very immodeſt in their words

and actions, and will often put the young men to the
blufh. The men commonly appear to be poffeffed of
much more modefty than the women; yet I have been
acquainted with fome young fquaws that appeared really
modeft: genuine it muft be, as they were under very
little reftraint in the channel of education or cuftom.

When the Indians meet one another, inftead of faying,
how do you do, they commonly falute in the following
manner—you are my friend—the reply is, truly friend,
I am your friend,—or, coufin, you yet exift—the reply
is certainly I do.—They have their children under tolerable command: feldom ever whip them, and their common mode of chaftifing, is by ducking them in cold
water; therefore their children are more obedient in the
winter feafon, than they are in the fummer; tho they
are then not fo often ducked. They are a peaceable
people, and fcarcely ever wrangle or fcold, when fober;
but they are very much addicted to drinking, and men
and women will become bafely intoxicated, if they can,
by any means, procure or obtain fpirituous liquor; and
then they are commonly either extremely merry and
kind, or very turbulent, ill-humoured and diforderly.

ON THEIR TRADITIONS AND RELIGIOUS
SENTIMENTS.

As the family that I was adopted into was intermarried with the Wiandots and Ottawas, three tongues were commonly fpoke, viz. Caughnewaga, or what the French call Iroque, alfo the Wiandot and Ottawa; by this means I had an opportunity of learning thefe three tongues; and I found that thefe nations varied in their traditions and opinions concerning religion;—and even numbers of the fame nations differed widely in their religious fentiments. Their traditions are vague, whimfical, romantic and many of them fcarce worth relating; and not any of them reach back to the creation of the world. The Wiandots comes the neareft to this. They tell of a fquaw that was found when an infant, in the water in a canoe made of bull-rufhes: this fquaw became a great prophetefs and did many wonderful things; fhe turned water into dry land, and at length made this continent, which was, at that time, only a very fmall ifland, and but a few Indians in it. Tho they were then but few they had not fufficient room to hunt; therefore this fquaw went to the water fide, and prayed that this little ifland might be enlarged. The great being then heard her prayer, and fent great numbers of

Water Tortoifes, and Mufkrats, which brought with them mud and other materials, for enlarging this ifland, and by this means, they fay, it was encreafed to the fize that it now remains; therefore they fay, that the white people ought not to encroach upon them, or take their land from them, becaufe their great grand mother made it.—They fay, that about this time the angels or heavenly inhabitants, as they call them, frequently vifited them and talked with their forefathers; and gave directions how to pray, and how to appeafe the great being when he was offended. They told them that they were to offer facrifice, burn tobacco, buffaloe and deer bones; but that they were not to burn bears or racoons bones in facrifice.

The Ottawas fay, that there are two great beings that rule and govern the univerfe, who are at war with each other; the one they call *Maneto*, and the other *Matchemaneto*. They fay that Maneto is all kindnefs and love, and that Matchemaneto is an evil fpirit, that delights in doing mifchief; and fome of them think, that they are equal in power, and therefore worfhip the evil fpirit out of a principle of fear. Others doubt which of the two may be the moft powerful, and therefore endeavor to keep in favor with both, by giving each of them fome kind of worfhip. Others fay that Maneto is the firft great caufe and therefore muft be all-powerful and fupreme, and ought to be adored and worfhipped; whereas Matchemaneto ought to be rejected and difpifed.

Thofe of the Ottawas that worfhip the evil fpirit, pretend to be great conjurors. I think if there is any fuch thing now in the world as witchcraft, it is among thefe people. I have been told wonderful ftories concerning their proceedings; but never was eye witnefs to any thing that appeared evidently fupernatural.

Some of the Wiandots and Caughnewagas profefs to be Roman-catholics; but even thefe retain many of the notions of their anceftors. Thofe of them who reject the Roman-catholic religion, hold that there is one great firft caufe, whom they call *Owaneeyo*, that rules and governs the univerfe, and takes care of all his creatures, rational and irrational, and gives them their food in due feafon, and hears the prayers of all thofe that call upon him; therefore it is but juft and reafonable to pray, and offer facrifice to this great being, and to do thofe things that are pleafing in his fight;—but they differ widely in what is pleafing or difpleafing to this great being. Some hold that following nature or their own propenfities is the way to happinefs, and cannot be difpleafing to the deity, becaufe he delights in the happinefs of his creatures, and does nothing in vain; but gave thefe difpofitions with a defign to lead to happinefs, and therefore they ought to be followed. Others reject this opinion altogether, and fay that following their own propenfities in this manner, is neither the means of happinefs nor the way to pleafe the deity.

Tecaughretanego was of opinion that following nature

in a limited fenfe was reafonable and right. He faid that moft of the irrational animals by following their natural propenfities, were led to the greateft pitch of happinefs that their natures and the world they lived in would admit of. He faid that mankind and the rattle fnakes had evil difpofitions, that led them to injure themfelves and others. He gave inftances of this. He faid he had a puppy that he did not intend to raife, and in order to try an experiment, he tyed this puppy on a pole and held it to a rattle fnake, which bit it feveral times; that he obferved the fnake fhortly after, rolling about apparently in great mifery, fo that it appeared to have poifoned itfelf as well as the puppy. The other in-ftance he gave was concerning himfelf. He faid that when he was a young man, he was very fond of the women, and at length got the venereal difeafe, fo that by following this propenfity, he was led to injure himfelf and others. He faid our happinefs depends on our ufing our reafon, in order to fupprefs thefe evil difpofitions; but when our propenfities neither lead us to injure ourfelves nor others, we might with fafety indulge them, or even pur-fue them as the means of happinefs.

The Indians generally are of opinion that there are great numbers of inferior Deities, which they call *Car-reyagaroona*, which fignifies the Heavenly Inhabitants. Thefe beings they fuppofe are employed as affiftants, in managing the affairs of the univerfe, and in infpecting the actions of men: and that even the irrational animals are engaged in viewing their actions, and bearing intelligence to the Gods. The eagle, for this purpose, with her keen eye, is soaring about in the day, and the owl, with her nightly eye, perched on the trees around their camp in the night; therefore, when they observe the eagle or the owl near, they immediately offer sacrifice, or burn tobacco, that they may have a good report to carry to the Gods. They say that there are also great numbers of evil spirits, which they call *Onasahroona*, which signifies the Inhabitants of the Lower Region. These they say are employed in disturbing the world, and the good spirits are always going after them, and setting things right, so that they are constantly working in opposition to each other. Some talk of a future state, but not with any certainty: at best their notions are vague and unsettled. Others deny a future state altogether, and say that after death they neither think or live.

As the Caughnewagas and the six nations speak nearly the same language, their theology is also nearly alike. When I met with the Shawanees or Delawares, as I could not speak their tongue, I spoke Ottawa to them, and as it bore some resemblance to their language, we understood each other in some common affairs, but as I could only converse with them very imperfectly, I can not from my own knowledge, with certainty, give any account of their theological opinions.

ON THEIR POLICE OR CIVIL GOVERN-MENT.

I have often heard of Indian Kings, but never faw any.—How any term ufed by the Indians in their own tongue, for the chief man of a nation, could be rendered King, I know not. The chief of a nation is neither a fupreme ruler, monarch or potentate—He can neither make war or peace, leagues or treaties—He cannot imprefs foldiers, or difpofe of magazines—He cannot adjourn, prorogue or diffolve a general affembly, nor can he refufe his affent to their conclufions, or in any manner controul them—With them there is no fuch thing as heriditary fucceffion, title of nobility or royal blood, even talked of—The chief of a nation, even with the confent of his affembly, or council, cannot raife one fhilling of tax off the citizens, but only receive what they pleafe to give as free and voluntary donations.— The chief of a nation has to hunt for his living, as any other citizen—How then can they with any propriety, be called kings? I apprehend that the white people were formerly fo fond of the name of kings, and fo ignorant of their power, that they concluded the chief man of a nation muft be a king.

As they are illiterate, they confequently have no written code of laws. What they execute as laws, are either old cuftoms, or the immediate refult of new councils. Some of their ancient laws or cuftoms are very pernicious, and difturb the public weal. Their vague law of marriage is a glaring inftance of this, as the man and his wife are under no legal obligation to live together, if they are both willing to part. They have little form, or ceremony among them, in matrimony, but do like the Ifraelites of old—the man goes in unto the woman, and fhe becomes his wife. The years of puberty and the age of confent, is about fourteen for the women, and eighteen for the men. Before I was taken by the Indians, I had often heard that in the ceremony of marriage, the man gave the woman a deer's leg, and fhe gave him a red ear of corn, fignifying that fhe was to keep him in bread, and he was to keep her in meat. I enquired of them concerning the truth of this, and they faid they knew nothing of it, further than that they had heard that it was the ancient cuftom among fome nations. Their frequent changing of partners prevents propagation, creates difturbances, and often occafions murder and bloodfhed; though this is commonly committed under pretenfe of being drunk. Their impunity to crimes committed when intoxicated with fpirituous liquors, or their admitting one crime as an excufe for another, is a very unjuft law or cuftom.

The extremes they run into in dividing the neceffaries of life, are hurtful to the public weal; though their dividing meat when hunting, may anfwer a valuable purpofe, as one family may have fuccefs one day, and the other the next; but their carrying this cuftom to the town, or to agriculture, is ftriking at the root of induftry, as induftrious perfons ought to be rewarded, and the lazy fuffer for their indolence.

They have fcarcely any penal laws: the principal punifhment is degrading: even murder is not punifhed by any formal law, only the friends of the murdered are at liberty to flay the murderer, if fome atonement is not made. Their not annexing penalties to their laws, is perhaps not as great a crime, or as unjuft and cruel, as the bloody penal laws of England, which we have fo long fhamefully practifed, and which are in force in this ftate, until our penitentiary houfe is finifhed, which is now building, and then they are to be repealed.

Let us alfo take a view of the advantages attending Indian police:—They are not oppreffed or perplexed with expenfive litigation—They are not injured by legal robbery—They have no fplendid villains that make themfelves grand and great on other people's labor—They have neither church or ftate erected as money-making machines.

ON THEIR DISCIPLINE, AND METHOD
OF WAR.

I have often heard the Britifh officers call the Indians the undifciplined favages, which is a capital miftake —as they have all the effentials of difcipline. They are under good command, and punctual in obeying orders: they can act in concert, and when their officers lay a plan and give orders, they will chearfully unite in putting all their directions into immediate execution ; and by each man obferving the motion or movement of his right hand companion, they can communicate the motion from right to left, and march abreaft in concert, and in fcattered order, though the line may be more than a mile long, and continue, if occafion requires, for a confiderable diftance, without diforder or confufion. They can perform various neceffary manœuvers, either flowly, or as faft as they can run : they can form a circle, or femi-circle : the circle they make ufe of, in order to furround their enemy, and the femi-circle if the enemy has a river on one fide of them. They can alfo form a large hollow fquare, face out and take trees : this they do, if their enemies are about furrounding them, to prevent from being fhot from either fide of the tree. When they go into battle they are not loaded or encumbered with many clothes, as they commonly fight naked, fave only breech-clout, leggins and mocke-fons. There is no fuch thing as corporeal punifhment ufed, in order to bring them under fuch good difcipline: degrading is the only chaftifement, and they are fo unanimous in this, that it effectually anfwers the purpofe. Their officers plan, order and conduct matters until they they are brought into action, and then each man is to fight as though he was to gain the battle himfelf. General orders are commonly given in time of battle; either to advance or retreat, and is done by a fhout or yell, which is well underftood, and then they retreat or advance in concert. They are generally well equipped, and exceeding expert and active in the ufe of arms. Could it be fuppofed that undifciplined troops could defeat Generals Braddock, Grant, &c? It may be faid by fome that the French were alfo engaged in this war: true, they were; yet I know it was the Indians that laid the plan, and with fmall affiftance, put it into execution. The Indians had no aid from the French, or any other power, when they befieged Fort Pitt in the year 1763, and cut off the communication for a confiderable time, between that poft and Fort Loudon, and would have defeated General Bouquet's army, (who were on the way to raife the fiege) had it not been for the affiftance of the Virginia volunteers. They had no Britifh troops with them when they defeated Colonel Crawford, near the Sandufky, in the time of the American War with Great Britain; or when they defeated Colonel Lough-rie, on the Ohio, near the Miami, on his way to meet General Clarke : this was alfo in the time of the Britifh war. It was the Indians alone that defeated Colonel Todd, in Kentucky, near the Blue licks, in the year 1782; and Colonel Harmer, betwixt the Ohio and Lake Erie, in the year 1790, and General St. Clair, in the year 1791; and it is faid that there was more of our men killed at this defeat, than there were in any one battle during our conteft with Great Britain. They had no aid when they fought even the Virginia rifle-men almoft a whole day, at the Great Kanhawa, in the year 1774; and when they found they could not prevail againft the Virginians, they made a moft artful retreat. Notwithftanding they had the Ohio to crofs, fome continued firing, whilft others were croffing the river; in this manner they proceeded until they all got over, before the Virginians knew that they had retreated; and in this retreat they carried off all their wounded. In the moft of the foregoing defeats, they fought with an inferior number, though in this, I believe it was not the cafe.

Nothing can be more unjuftly reprefented than the different accounts we have had of their number from time to time, both by their own computations, and that of the Britifh. While I was among them, I faw the account of the number, that they in thofe parts gave to the French, and kept it by me. When they in their own council-houfe, were taking an account of their number, with a piece of bark newly ftripped, and a fmall ftick, which anfwered the end of a flate and pencil, I took an account of the different nations and tribes, which I added together, and found there were not half the number which they had given the French; and though they were then their allies, and lived among them, it was not eafy finding out the deception, as they were a wandering fet, and fome of them almoft always in the woods hunting. I afked one of the chiefs what was their reafon for making fuch different returns? He faid it was for political reafons, in order to obtain greater prefents from the French, by telling them they could not divide fuch and fuch quantities of goods among fo many.

In year of General Bouquet's laft campaign, 1764, I faw the official return made by the Britifh officers, of the number of Indians that were in arms againft us that year, which amounted to thirty thoufand. As I was then a lieutenant in the Britifh fervice, I told them I was of opinion that there was not above one thoufand in arms againft us, as they were divided by Broadftreet's army being then at Lake Erie. The Britifh officers hooted at me, and faid they could not make England fenfible of the difficulties they labored under in fighting them, as England expects that their troops could fight the undifciplined favages in America, five to one, as

20

they did the Eaſt-Indians, and therefore my report
would not anſwer their purpoſe, as they could not give
an honorable account of the war, but by augmenting
their number. I am of opinion that from Braddock's
war, until the preſent time, there never were more than
three thouſand Indians at any time, in arms againſt us,
weſt of Fort Pitt, and frequently not half that number.
According to the Indians' own accounts during the
whole of Braddock's war, or from 1755, till 1758, they
killed or took, fifty of our people, for one that they
loſt. In the war that commenced in the year 1763, they
killed, comparatively, few of our people, and loſt more
of theirs, as the frontiers (eſpecially the Virginians) had
learned ſomething of their method of war : yet, they,
in this war, according to their own accounts, (which I
believe to be true) killed or took ten of our people, for
one they loſt.

Let us now take a view of the blood and treaſure that
was ſpent in oppoſing comparatively, a few Indian warriors, with only ſome aſſiſtance from the French, the firſt
four years of the war. Additional to the amazing de-
ſtruction and ſlaughter that the frontiers ſuſtained, from
James River to Suſquehanna, and about thirty miles
broad; the following campaigns were alſo carried on
againſt the Indians:—General Braddock's, in the year
1755: Colonel Armſtrong's againſt the Cattanyan town,
on the Alleghany, 1757: General Forbes', in 1758:
General Stanwick's, in 1759: General Monkton's, in

1760: Colonel Bouquet's, 1761—and 1763, when he fought the battle of Bufhy Run, and loft above one hundred men ; but by the affiftance of the Virginia volunteers, drove the Indians; Colonel Armftrong's, up the Weft Branch of Susquehanna, in 1763: General Broadftreet's, up Lake Erie, in 1764: General Bouquet's, againft the Indians at Mufkingum, in 1764: Lord Dunmore's, in 1774: General M'Intofh's, in 1778 : Colonel Crawford's, fhortly after his, General Clarke's in 1778—1780: Colonel Bowman's, 1779: General Clarke's, in 1782—againft the Wabafh, in 1786: General Logan's againft the Shawanees in 1786: General Wilkinfon's in ——: Colonel Harmer's in 1790: and General St. Clair's, in 1791; which, in all, are twenty-two campaigns, befides fmaller expeditions, fuch as the French Creek expedition, Colonels Edward's, Loughrie's, &c. All thefe were exclufive of the number of men that were internally employed as fcouting parties, and in erecting forts, guarding ftations, &c. When we take the foregoing occurrences into confideration, may we not reafonably conclude, that they are the beft difciplined troops in the known world? Is it not the beft difcipline that has the greateft tendency to annoy the enemy and fave their own men? I apprehend that the Indian difcipline is as well calculated to anfwer the purpofe in the woods of America, as the Britifh difcipline in Flanders : and Britifh difcipline in the woods, is the way to have men flaughtered, with fcarcely any chance of defending themfelves.

Let us take a view of the benefits we have received, by what little we have learned of their art of war, which coft us dear, and the lofs that we have fuftained for want of it, and then fee if it will not be well worth our while to retain what we have, and alfo to endeavor to improve in this neceffary branch of bufinefs. Though we have made confiderable proficiency in this line, and in fome refpects out-do them, *viz.* as markfmen, and in cutting our rifles, and in keeping them in good order; yet, I apprehend we are far behind in their manœuvres, or in being able to furprize, or prevent a furprize. May we not conclude that the progrefs we had made in their art of war, contributed confiderably towards our fuccefs, in various refpects, when contending with great Britain for liberty? Had the Britifh king, attempted to enflave us before Braddock's war, in all probability he might readily have done it, becaufe, except the New-Englanders, who had formerly been engaged in war, with the Indians, we were unacquainted with any kind of war: but after fighting fuch a fubtil and barbarous enemy as the Indians, we were not terrified at the approach of Britifh red-coats.—Was not Burgoyne's defeat accomplifhed in fome meafure by the Indian mode of fighting? and did not Gen. Morgan's rifle-men, and many others, fight with greater fuccefs, in confequence of what they had learned of their art of war? Kentucky would not have been fettled at the time it was, had the Virginians been altogether ignorant of this method of war.

In Braddock's war, the frontiers were laid wafte, for above three hundred miles long, and generally about thirty broad, excepting fome that were living in forts, and many hundreds, or perhaps thoufands, killed or made captives, and horfes, and all kinds of property carried off: but, in the next Indian war, though we had the fame Indians to cope with, the frontiers almoft all ftood their ground, becaufe they were by this time, in fome meafure acquainted with their manœvres; and the want of this, in the firft war, was the caufe of the lofs of many hundred of our citizens, and much treafure.

Though large volumes have been wrote on morality, yet it may all be fummed up in faying, do as you would wifh to be done by: fo the Indians fum up the art of war in the following manner:

The bufinefs of the private warriors is to be under command, or punctually to obey orders—to learn to march a-hreaft in fcattered order, fo as to be in readinefs to furround the enemy, or to prevent being furrounded —to be good markfmen, and active in the ufe of arms— to practice running—to learn to endure hunger or hard-fhips with patience and fortitude—to tell the truth at all times to their officers, but more efpecially when fent out to fpy the enemy.

Concerning Officers. They fay that it would be abfurd to appoint a man an officer whofe fkill and courage had never been tried—that all officers fhould be advanced only according to merit—that no one man fhould have the abfolute command of an army—that a council of officers are to determine when, and how an attack is to be made—that it is the bufinefs of the officers to lay plans to take every advantage of the enemy—to ambufh and furprize them, and to prevent being ambufhed and furprized themfelves—it is the duty of officers to prepare and deliver fpeeches to the men, in order to annimate and encourage them; and on the march, to prevent the men, at any time, from getting into a huddle, becaufe if the enemy fhould furround them in this pofition, they would be expofed to the enemy's fire. It is likewife their bufinefs at all times to endeavor to annoy their enemy, and fave their own men, and therefore ought never to bring on an attack without confiderable advantage, or without what appeared to them the fure profpect of victory, and that with the lofs of few men: and if at any time they fhould be miftaken in this, and are like to lofe many men by gaining the victory, it is their duty to retreat, and wait for a better opportunity of defeating their enemy, without the danger of lofing fo many men. Their conduct proves that they act upon thefe principles, therefore it is, that from Braddock's war to the prefent time, they have feldom ever made an unfuccefsful attack. The battle at the mouth of the Great Kanhawa, is the greateft inftance of this; and even then, though the Indians killed about three, for one they loft, yet they retreated. The lofs of the Virginians in this action, was feventy killed and the fame number wounded:—The Indians loſt twenty killed on the field, and eight, who died afterwards, of their wounds. This was the greateſt loſs of men that I ever knew the Indians to ſuſtain in any one battle. They will commonly retreat if their men are falling faſt—they will not ſtand cutting, like the Highlanders, or other Britiſh troops: but this proceeds from a compliance with their rules of war, rather than cowardice. If they are ſurrounded, they will fight while there is a man of them alive, rather than ſurrender. When Colonel John Armſtrong ſurrounded the Cattanyan town, on the Allegheny river, Captain Jacobs, a Delaware chief, with ſome warriors, took poſſeſſion of a houſe, defended themſelves for ſome time, and killed a number of our men. As Jacobs could ſpeak Engliſh, our people called on him to ſurrender: he ſaid that he and his men were warriors, and they would all fight while life remained. He was again told that they ſhould be well uſed, if they would only ſurrender; and if not, the houſe ſhould be burned down over their heads:—Jacobs replied he could eat fire: and when the houſe was in a flame, he, and they that were with him, came out in a fighting poſition, and were all killed. As they are a ſharp, active kind of people, and war is their principal ſtudy, in this they have arrived at conſiderable perfection. We may learn of the Indians what is uſeful and laudable, and at the ſame time lay aſide their barbarous proceedings. It is much to be lamented that ſome of our frontier rifle-men

are prone to imitate them in their inhumanity.   During
the Britifh war, a confiderable number of men from below Fort Pitt, croffed the Ohio, and marched into a
town of Friendly Indians, chiefly Delawares, who profeffed the Moravian religion.   As the Indians apprehended no danger, they neither lifted arms or fled.
After thefe rifle-men were fometime in the town, and
the Indians altogether in their power, in cool blood,
they maffacred the whole town, without diftinction of
age or fex.   This was an act of barbarity beyond any
thing I ever knew to be committed by the favages themfelves.

Why have we not made greater proficiency in the
Indian art of war?   Is it becaufe we are too proud to
imitate them, even though it fhould be a means of pre-
ferving the lives of many of our citizens?   No!   We
are not above borrowing language from them, fuch as
homony, pone, tomahawk, &c. which is little or no ufe
to us.   I apprehend that the reafons why we have not
improved more in this refpect, are as follows: no important acquifition is to be obtained but by attention
and diligence; and as it is eafier to learn to move and
act in concert, in clofe order, in the open plain, than to
act in concert in fcattered order, in the woods; fo it is
eafier to learn our difcipline, than the Indian manœuvres.
They train up their boys to the art of war from the
time they are twelve or fourteen years of age; whereas
the principal chance our people had of learning, was by

obferving their movements when in action againft us. I have been long aftonifhed that no one has wrote upon this important fubject, as their art of war would not only be of ufe to us in cafe of another rupture with them ; but were only part of our men taught this art, accompanied with our continental difcipline, I think no European power, after trial, would venture to fhew its head in the American woods.

If what I have wrote fhould meet the approbation of my countrymen, perhaps I may publifh more upon this fubject, in a future edition.

END.